For Nigel and Mark

PETER ROBINS

OUR HERO HAS BAD BREATH

Brilliance Books

This collection first published by Brilliance Books 1982
Brilliance Books 110 Glenthorne Road London W6 England

Typeset by MC Typeset, Rochester
Printed in Great Britain by Nene Litho
and bound by Woolnough Bookbinding
both of Wellingborough, Northants

Some of these stories have appeared (often in earlier drafts) in :
The Gay Journal, Gay News, Gold, Christopher Street (U.S.A.),
Paragraph (U.S.A.), Revolt (Sweden), The Libertine (Australia)
Spartacus (Holland), One has also been broadcast on Capital
Radio London England.

CONTENTS

PETER ROBINS

OUR HERO HAS BAD BREATH

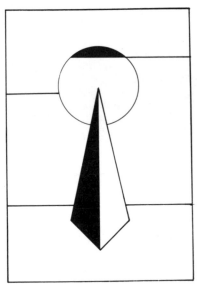

Brilliance Books

GREEN GEORGE

Old Mr Clamber's walking stick had been removed. Ethel's umbrella was a couple of shades less funereal than Mrs Clamber's had been. Such changes excepted, the hall stand on which Edward placed his brief case was just as it had been when he had played hide-and-seek around it as a child.

Number 4, Wren Grove – which Edward partly owned – had not altered much either. Longer worsted trousers and shorter sight apart, some wondered whether Edward himself had changed much since adolescence. Certainly the notion occurred to Ethel – and not for the first time – as she heard him pad across the sitting room behind her one evening in April. A moment later, as Edward paused between Ethel and the French windows before leaning down to kiss her, he realised how much his wife had altered. Not yet twenty eight, she appeared quite wan and wasted.

Edward, loosening his Rotarian's tie, glanced back at the garden.

'Turned out quite nice, didn't it, after that unpromising start? You know it was really quite sticky coming along from the station. Closed these doors early this evening, didn't you, old stick?'

'Edward, that hedge moved an hour ago. I'm watching to see if it moves again.'

Now Edward, being a Civil Servant who was indispensable to his Permanent Secretary, always evaluated the untoward dispassionately. He considered whether (a) Ethel might at last be pregnant or (b) that she might be manifesting early those oddities and quirks to which her elder relatives seemed prone.

'Beg pardon, my dear, did you say . . .?'

'Edward, I am not being emotional.' (She emphasised this by smacking the dralon arm of the chair with the flat of her hand.)

'That laurel hedge was moving. There was a face peering from the leaves. It grinned towards this room and I'm terrified. Do something, Edward.'

He did. He poured a sherry for them both and, as he did so, improvised some logical explanations. The incident might (a) have been a trick of the evening light or (b) Ethel might need glasses as a result of poring perpetually over her flower embroideries or (c), and much more probable, a tramp might have been passing.

Ethel, more certain than before that her husband's common-sense began and ended with the departmental memoranda that he left in his brief case each night, said nothing but continued to stare into the thickening shadows under the apple blossom. Leaving her sherry half finished she went to the kitchen to fetch their trays of cod and mushroom pie.

Her screams had Edward sprinting as nimbly into action as he did when the Permanent Secretary coughed. Their supper, or what remained of it, was on the table. A wooden spoon stood erect in the uneaten portion. The usually spotless black and white floor tiles were spattered with clay clods and they both counted five laurel leaves by the open door.

'Now, now, old girl, simmer down. This just about clinches the matter. It is, as I suspected, a hungry tramp.'

'Who's probably still lurking. Edward, you must call the police. We're not safe in our own home.'

'No,' he replied emphatically, 'not yet. I shall handle this.' And he fetched his father's old ashplant from under the stairs. That he was somewhat agitated despite the cool exterior can be guessed since he made first for the hall stand, quite forgetting old Mr Clamber had been dead ten years.

The sun was setting over the Bingo Hall as Ethel watched Edward striding across the patio, over the lawn he tended so lovingly each weekend and into the orchard. Because she could

12

still see him and because her husband turned sharply – having heard it also – Ethel was less appalled by the bellow of laughter that erupted from their sitting room than she would otherwise have been.

With Edward once more beside her they crept, a little breathlessly, through the unlit hall. He relied on the ashplant and common-sense and she depended – none too confidently – on him. There was no masked intruder at the china cabinet; no hobgoblin perched on the what-not. Nor did there seem to be any evidence of disruption until Ethel screamed, 'My handbag.'

She checked the contents littering the carpet and there was only a lipstick missing.

'Quite impossible,' Edward asserted, 'you've left it upstairs. That was a man's laugh we heard.'

They also heard a muffled giggle somewhere behind them and then a click as the front door was pulled from the outside.

'Edward,' Ethel trembled, 'he was in the hall. I mean just now. We might have passed him as we came in here. Do you realise he could have *touched* me?'

When the wall-lights were switched on, all was as it had been for the five years of their married life except that a lipstick was on the rug by the hall stand and, across the mirror was scrawled, 'The Green Gang Was Here.'

Ethel, as she read it, giggled less hysterically than might have been expected.

'Your tramp is rather sophisticated,' she said.

Edward, reviewing the locked French windows and the open kitchen door concluded the intruder must have had a key. There was but one solution – George was back.

'I think we'd better come and sit down, old stick,' (he was guiding Ethel to a kitchen chair as he spoke), 'I fear I know who it is. Brother George is in the vicinity again . . . yes, yes dear, I know it's been all of seven years but he's the only one who could have a set of keys. Remember I could never change the locks? The house is half his whatever we say.'

Ethel twisted her wedding ring, a habit that irritated Edward.

Finally she said, 'I'm not staying here if that man is going to have regular access. None of your family would ever tell me what he did. If you ask me there's not much he hasn't done by now. I expect he's an alcoholic. From what I've pieced together I should think he's a communist and I've no doubt he's riddled with one of those social diseases they advertise in the lavatories. We must go to a hotel for the night.'

Edward, however, had no intention of ceding such ground as he held. His half share of the house wasn't much but to him it was all. Having negotiated over several pots of tea, he managed to get Ethel to accept that the intrusion had really only resulted in the loss of half a cod and mushroom pie. By midnight she had helped him wedge furniture against the door and, by half past, they were snuggled into their twin divans where they slept fitfully.

'I trust,' Edward observed over breakfast, 'everything will be as near normal as possible today. Lunch, as I mentioned earlier, could well be the turning point in my career.'

'What about the stability of our marriage, Edward? Let me tell you that your brother's arrival could very well prove a turning-point in that. O yes, I'll make avocado mousse for your wretched Permanent Secretary but – mark my words – I want out so far as this house is concerned.'

'Let's not get emotional old thing. Look, I'll go to the super-market for you.'

At least, Ethel consoled herself, he'd not be fussing at her elbow while she cooked lunch.

Perhaps an hour later, well, at some critical moment over the stove, the doorbell rang. 'Damn,' hissed Ethel, grabbing her purse. The milkman had a knack of arriving just when one could do without him. 'You're early for once,' she began.

It was most certainly not the milkman but Ethel knew who it must be. Brother George was technicolour to Edward's black and white. It was not a face one finds in offices. He'd a pale green polo necked jersey, stained and patched. From a foot away, Ethel caught the raw tang of his sweat. It fascinated her in a shocking way and she felt rather as she had done when Edward, drunk one

Christmas, had kissed her, well, down there. George's eyes, she noticed, were as brown as Edward's though George's had sparklers behind them.

'Didn't want to bust in and give you palpitations,' he smiled, striding past Ethel, who realised she was clutching the knocker.

'Our Teddy not at home then? Not out chatting up the birds is he?' He was already in the sitting room, dragging off his boots to reveal grimed mountaineering socks and – through a constellation of holes – grimier feet.

'Right then. Going to make a nice milky drink for me eh, love? I could just tackle something warm and nourishing.'

As he glanced her over, Ethel felt that coarse fingers sprouted from his eyes, fondling her. She forced herself to concentrate on what he was saying.

'. . . and then, Ethel dearest, I'd like a little kip. Been on an all night frolic you understand.'

'We like our guests to let us know when they're coming and going, George. Certainly I'll make some coffee and I suppose you could rest in one of our guest rooms. There is one that used to be yours.' Recalling that she was talking to the co-owner of the house she flushed as she threw in awkwardly, 'But you'll remember where that is, won't you?'

The harsh smell of burning vegetables sent her scurrying to the kitchen. From there she conveyed to Edward, when he returned from the shopping precinct, that George was entrenched in the sitting room. Her mime was punctuated with references to her wrist-watch for, in far less than a hour, the Permanent Secretary would arrive. That was not a prospect to which Ethel thrilled anyway. Over her embroidery she wondered increasingly if anything ever would.

Through the open doors she could hear her husband's voice.

'Well, George . . . long time no see. What can we do for you?'

'There's a home-coming. Do I have to fill in a form to visit my own place of residence?'

'Only half yours,' Edward snapped almost gleefully. Chancing how far his savings account and bank manager would back him he continued, 'I'd always be willing to buy you out . . .'

Ethel, who'd taken in a cup of coffee, was totally unprepared for George to thank her by patting her bottom. She skipped to Edward's side and hovered, ready for further flight, yet eager to witness any acceptance of her husband's proposition.

'You bet your manky pension you would. And then what would the two of you do with all this space? I don't feel you've been doing your duty, our Teddy. Eight years married almost and no kiddie-winkies. There should be a platoon of little grey Teddies by now all conditioned to defend your concrete city . . .'

'That's very offensive,' chirped Ethel.

'Damned personal, I'd say,' chorused Edward, 'but I choose to ignore it. Now, George, what do you say? A fair valuation; cash in hand and you leave us alone . . . for good.'

'I'm tempted,' mused George putting down his cup and farting slowly, 'I see the thought of being rid of me defrosting your eyes already, little Ted. Alternatively,' he yawned, 'I could exercise my right to half of everything. I might well move in here with some of the Green Gang.' He eased his greasy hand against one of Ethel's embroidered cushions. 'You could hardly evict your own twin. Not at present . . . though . . . must say . . . way things are shaping in . . . this dear old land of ours . . .'

He showed every sign of dozing off and, as Edward turned to whisper to Ethel, a counterpoint of snores began.

'Leave him. We'll take the Permanent Secretary onto the patio after lunch. I'll go and keep a weather-eye open for him otherwise the doorbell will rouse this incubus.'

Edward explained to his boss that the sitting room was being redecorated and led him immediately to the dining room. Ethel, who had drawn the sitting room curtains and popped on her shoes to welcome the visitor, poured sherries for them all and scurried to the kitchen, leaving the men to talk business. All was tranquil at Number 4, Wren Grove as it was at Number 2 where grandfather (who was a bishop) was being entertained; and at Number 6, where a lightweight champion was discussing with his masseur who should go down and make breakfast.

16

When the Permanent Secretary accepted a second portion of Ethel's quiche she was touched. Edward, pressing on to success, topped up the hock. As their guest was murmuring, 'We do both realise – we all realise for that matter, the delicacy of the whole project. We base our thinking on a hypothetical nuclear crisis. Hence the need for a co-ordinating committee and that . . . Edward · . . . is where you . . .' George strolled in.

He had helped himself to Edward's razor and was looking healthier than ever after his brief nap. His hair had been combed and the brown-gold curls twinkled in what light outwitted the heavy net curtains. He'd not sponged his stained jersey but must have been foraging upstairs for old Mrs Clamber's cornelian brooch had been pinned to it.

'Hello again,' he grinned and hooked three fingersful of mousse from the centre bowl. 'Been hiding me from the guest of honour, then?'

The guest stared. Edward stared. Neither spoke.

'There is a spoon George,' Ethel ventured, inspecting the surface of her reproduction Regency oak table.

'But is any spoon long enough I ask myself?' George mused as he ambled round to the Permanent Secretary, licking each finger in turn. Holding the nonplussed man lightly by the chin, George began to chuckle so that the white webs on either side of his eyes were lost in his over-all tan. 'So who are you, handsome?' he asked.

Ethel, who had been about to weep at the ruin of her lunch (hostesses tended to do just that in such novels as she skimmed) unaccountably began to giggle. Edward took charge.

'Would you care to join us? This is George – my brother. George – the Permanent Secretary, Sir Noseworthy Cheeseworth.'

'Astounding name,' George whistled, not moving from where he stood. Matching action to words he went on, 'if you chucked away these glasses and ruffled your mop with a gutful of clean breeze, know something? I'd quite fancy you.'

'My brother,' interjected Edward, 'attempts to outrage us on those very rare occasions we meet. He alleges he had some experience on a mountaineering holiday seven years ago.

Certainly he's never been the same since.'

'Too right old dear,' (George was lightly drumming Sir Noseworthy's skull) 'nor was anyone else on the trip either.'

The Permanent Secretary stood up, retrieved his glasses from the bread basket and snapped them into their case.

'I am not,' he observed with a finality that had flattened leading politicians in many a government, 'attracted to men in the slightest.'

'I'm so relieved,' said George with some concern, 'no civil servant should get sexy about anything but rules and precedents.'

'Edward, Mrs Clamber . . . I take the view that I should not intrude further on your little family reunion.'

'Sit down, Nosey — I'm going to.' George thrust the unhappy man back into the chair. 'Now listen. Don't go shuffling away with the idea that I want to prise our Teddy's toes off the pyramid of success. Cautious as a reptile and blameless as a corpse he can scramble after your cast-off shoes for all I care. Shall I tell you why I'm here? To remind these two they don't shit little bits of toffee. Have to give old Ted a nudge now and again, see? The house isn't all his you know. I'm his unsmotherable twin.' He patted Sir Noseworthy's sleeve. 'Bet you never dreamed of coming face to face with one of the Green Gang, eh? Must be quite a little bonus for you, meeting me. We exist alright — not just graffiti in your nightmares.' Noticing that Ethel was staring at him fascinated, he twitched his eyebrow lecherously. 'And what's biting you, darling? Of course, I should have guessed . . . it's the sex-bit, isn't it? Fret not, I won't ravish your kids. Damn, that was tactless — there aren't any, are there?' Pulling the salad bowl to him he continued, munching and chatting simultaneously. 'Ethel, I might have made out with you for a bit if Teddy bear hadn't gone picnicking first. And if I had, let me tell you, you wouldn't be looking like a textbook on anaemia. Mind you, I stray a bit: the occasional fisherman or market lad from time to time. I fear you might be the possessive type, our Ethel.'

'Where exactly do you live?' Sir Noseworthy, one could tell, had it in mind and in glance to initiate a discreet enquiry or two. The

Vagrancy Act, Broadmoor, the Pillory and Smithfield all glimmered in that look.

'Here and there, round and about,' George chuckled through a lettuce leaf. 'Squats . . . communes – that sort of thing. Fairgrounds or beaches in the summer. Winter draws us nearer the lights. We're never too far away.'

Sir Noseworthy asked if he might visit the cloakroom.

Edward rounded on his brother in a voice alternately shrill and profound, uncontrollable as that of a fourteen year old boy.

'What the bloody hell are you trying to do George? Do you loathe me so much, upsetting my wife (actually Ethel had never looked more lively since her wedding morning), ruining my prospects at the Ministry and kicking up no end of a scandal in a decent neighbourhood?'

'Cool it Teddy. As I explained, I'm here to remind you that you can't legislate me out of existence. I'm like the erection you get – well, maybe you do – in the middle of the vicarage fête. You don't understand, do you? Well, I'm the dandelions that heave up those neat stones on your patio. Our patio. I'm your uncouth twin, mate. We are the same flesh and blood aren't we? Not that you appear to have much blood left . . . but the flesh, Teddy, that's more ticklish, isn't it?' He glanced towards the Permanent Secretary who had returned but remained in the doorway, 'Well now that the Head Corpse is back from fingering himself, I'll be off.' He kissed both his relatives on the mouth and blew a third kiss to their guest as Sir Noseworthy leapt aside, allowing him to pass. From the hall he delivered a personal postscript to the Permanent Secretary.

'I would take the view that Edward is one of yours. Keep papering over the ugly cracks both of you. Not that your crumbling world can win, finally, any more than the rebels. The fun's in the trying though – if you take the thrust of my argument. You must let me know, Nosey, the going rate for a knighthood. I might sell my half of the house to Teddy and buy one on the proceeds . . .'

They watched him cross the front lawn, saw him grab a bud from an adventurous rose and thatch it into his hair. They stared as he ignored the wrought-iron gates and thrust, instead, through the laurel hedge bordering Number 4.

Sir Noseworthy was already peering towards the clock when Edward turned. He quickly moved towards Ethel, 'What about coffee?' When she had gone, Edward closed the door and said, 'I wouldn't add to that inexcusable scene other than to say that not even my wife knows, far less George, that the family never quite cleared up the matter of a mix-up in the maternity ward.'

'I believe I understand what you are saying Edward. Tell me, had it ever crossed your mind that you might move to that new block reserved for the Department? The one in the specially patrolled area? I would take the view that such a decision might be most appropriate.'

They forgot the incident – or seemed to – concentrating instead on office trivia. When they had dissected all their immediate colleagues with gentlemanly skill, Edward went out to the hall and called breezily, 'How are things doing, dear?'

There was no reply. The garden door was open and the coffee percolating. Edward sensed some subtle change. Putting on his glasses he noticed, on the white tiles at his feet, pink rosebuds – neat as any embroidery – outlined in lipstick.

There was no one in the garden. Edward was certain it was nothing but a ripple of wind that disturbed the laurel hedge.

He stood on the patio for some minutes calling, 'Ethel; Ethel.' There was a blurred rumble from lorries on the motorway. Birds gossiped in the apple trees and, nearer still, a rag-and-bone man yelled in the lane. Then the laughter began. Children's voices topped the rasping baritone of the rag man and the sound echoed over Wren Drive like exuberant bells.

Edward noticed the young boxer and his masseur laughing together from an upper window of Number 6 and pointing at the roof. He was aware that the Bishop had wandered into the garden of Number 2 and was glaring skywards like an outraged scarlet and mauve fuschia. Around him grandchildren were staring, too, but they were chuckling.

Edward moved over the flagstones to see for himself what had perched on his roof. Ethel, naked against the chimney stack, was laughing and waving over the front lawns and across the valley.

Edward was so petrified with horror and shame that no alternative courses of action occurred to him. His single thought was that Ethel might have used a laurel leaf to cover herself, at least, down there.

Note: the name Noseworthy Cheeseworth is not as improbable as may be thought. The Registrar for the Alphington District of Exeter in the 1830s who recorded the birth of my great-grandfather was the Rev Noseworthy Cheeseworth.

THE BRIDE OF DEATH

Almost everyone thought Ella prudent to have booked an alarm call for five thirty. Those who had known her for six decades shrugged, smiling, as if to say, 'What would you expect of Ella Thompson?' Given the advantage of that early start, the next couple of hours still seemed to evaporate as she took a bath, manicured her nails, slipped into a working-smock and had an occasional peek at the orchids in the fridge. By eight o'clock she was already thirty two minutes behind schedule. The grilled mushrooms and fried bananas she had planned had to be abandoned for a mere gesture of lemon juice and dry toast. Even then, she'd barely a moment to pop her head into the second bedroom to see how Ralph was before the hairdresser's assistant was thumping at the garden door to give her a shampoo and set.

Now Ella had anticipated a taxing day but the speed with which the morning was spinning away would have nonplussed any lesser stagemanager. The hairdresser's girl had not quite finished when an unusual relay race began. The two teams were supplied by Interflora and the Post Office telegraph boys. From Ella's wrought-iron gate to her oak-veneered Tudor door those runners plied with such frequency (each lap marked by a clang of the tubular bells) that long before ten she tired of meeting them and left the door open to let in the September morning. The front lawn was already a pleasing prospect: lane on lane of sheaves, wreaths and chaplets which had transformed the scabby grass to the cover of a Nursery Gardener's catalogue.

The house (bought long since in Ella's name with a bachelor uncle's legacy) faced the bitter coastline's one sweep of memorable sand. It was a villa that suited the landscape well – tall, gaunt and with the widowed look of a late Victorian methodist. It was set in a corner plot and, from the side lane where boarding houses huddled away from the wind, families replete with bacon and eggs began to dawdle towards the unattractive esplanade. They faltered by the low stone wall of *Dunromin* entraced by the florists' technicolour fantasies. Few could resist immortalising the moment with their cameras. All this Ella watched unnoticed through the amber glass of a landing window. Thoughtfully she had opened the door of the second bedroom so that she could give Ralph a detailed commentary.

Hearing footsteps across the gravel below she excused herself and trotted down hoping it might be one or other of her nephews reporting for the rehearsal. It was Joan, however, the home-help who called, 'Lovely morning you've got for it, Mrs T.,'

Lovely or not there was no time for chit-chat about September being the wine of the year. Lumpish Joan was directed to sorting cups and glasses in the lounge while their own mid-morning tea was brewing. And none too soon either. Guests (well, what else could one call them?) were beginning to converge from a dozen counties. Most wore black, many propelled themselves on sticks but all were bowed if not with grief then certainly with flowers: chrysanthemums and arum lilies, garnet roses and carnations jostled in overblown profusion. Immediate family were instructed to unload to the left. Mere colleagues and acquaintances added to the sparser rows towards the lane. Exchanging their garlands for cups of tea or supermarket sherry these early mourners picked their way among the tributes to price each other's offerings or to guess whose imagination might have conjured up a dwarf grand piano of assorted zinnias.

The two expected nephews arrived late but together. Ed, who peddled frozen foods, had a car that matched the job and his wife's aspirations. By chance they had caught up with John sauntering along the lane from the station. Having placed their flowers in the few remaining vacant inches, John and Ed furtively discussed the fitness of lighting cigarettes. No chance. Ella was scurrying towards them, at one glance assessing their regard for Ralph from the size of their offerings. The twelve crimson gladioli could only be from John. He had taste. Ella grudgingly admitted that, though she could never really care for him and sensed he laughed at her. As if being the Chief Cashier at a city bank gave him cause to think himself a cut above the rest of the family, she always said.

Her welcome to him – as to Ed and Vi – was less than a nod. She reminded them tersely that it was already twelve minutes to twelve and that the rehearsal would have to be pared back to brief instructions. Even these were interrupted by a tiresome man from the funeral parlour. Quite impudent he had been, Ella said later, to have accosted her in front of everybody.

'Now, Mrs Thompson, I've done all that I can. You mustn't take offence but I think you've been a naughty girl again. After Tuesday's little accident I did stress you shouldn't go on feeding your dear husband with tit-bits of ham sandwich . . .'

'Perhaps you'd just remember that he was my husband. If I can't pop in to let him know what's happening it's a fine thing I'm sure. He always enjoyed a nice bit of ham twice a week, did my Ralph. I refuse to be upset today of all days.'

'I've no wish to distress you further but I must insist Mrs Thompson that in this weather further repair work would be very difficult. Now I do hope you'll let him be until we leave for the church.'

'I do not intend to waste the next hour bandying words with you. Kindly go and pour yourself a sherry in the kitchen and leave me to my grief.'

John Thompson, having listened dumbly to the interchange, grabbed a sherry in each fist and balanced himself on the lip of an ornamental wishing well. Half-forgotten figures from his childhood limped about him. He smiled at them vaguely and began to stack his empties in the shadow of a plastic mermaid. By remaining unobtrusive he hoped to elude Ella and her repeated invitations to go into the house. Corpses did not unnerve him. Occasional visits to his uncle during the man's too-brief retirement schooled him for what others were being shown. Ralph, he had long decided, had been all but dead on arrival in Simscombe. Only skin and bone had remained animate. Grinding the stub of his cigarette into an arum lily John grunted at the mermaid, 'You should be a bloody bridesmaid. What d'you think of Ella's second wedding day, eh?'

The official photographers arrived and went briskly into action. Conversations dwindled to a murmur, punctuated every fifteen minutes by Ella clapping her hands on the front step to signify that another guided tour of the corpse was about to begin. Through open windows above the knots of in-laws and country cousins Ella's voice bore down more dominant than the distant crashing of the tide.

'You haven't seen him since Wednesday, have you? He's been looking very peaceful these past couple of days . . . I'm glad you agree the wax candles make all the difference. They do throw up the jewel colours in the new curtains, don't they? Yes, picked them up in Harrods the day before yesterday . . . oh, a cheap-day ticket of course – we widows must watch our pennies, you know.'

Ella clapped her hands with extra vehemence at one o'clock. This was the signal for John and Ed to leave for St Margaret's and for Ella herself to slip away and change.

There was a first spit of rain on the windscreen as Ed parked the car. As the two cousins loaded themselves with a couple of hundred printed Orders Of Service John muttered, 'What do we ask the gathering masses – friend of the heroine or the corpse?'

Ed, who recalled his wife's caution as well as her ambition, was not going to have Ella knocked. Enough hints had been scattered in conversations about young marrieds finding funds for a house deposit and it was to be hoped that Ralph might have altered his Will.

'C'mon, John man. If this is how she wants to . . . O.K. No sense in getting heavy eh? Ella and Ralph were both show-biz types so let's give him a fabulous gig.'

Show-biz thought John, though he merely shrugged, was the last thing Ralph would have wished to be. Hadn't he giggled with

John over the Ladies' Guild dreadful productions in which Ella involved herself: adenoidal Carmens and Romeos with unconcealable mammaries? Publicly loyal to his wife, John knew his uncle would have preferred retirement in a London garden or afternoons rummaging the second-hand shops. As Ed moved away, assuming a salesman's smile, John halted him. 'You may think it show-biz. To me it's bloody travelling circus.' The smile hardened.

'Now listen man. Just ask, "Friend of Ella or Ralph". No hassle eh?'

In twos and threes and then in dozens the congregation wandered in. Four dozen bright and purposeful women disgorged themselves from one coach alone. Though not in costume, the thespians of the Ladies' Guild weighed Ella's side of the nave too conspicuously to achieve any final balance. On Ralph's side there were representatives of the factory pension scheme. Their purpose, John supposed, as he led them to a pew, would be to attest that there had been a burial and the widow's half-pension might safely be paid. As he returned to the West door, he saw a man of about sixty, neat in grey, slip into the back row.

'You're a friend or colleague of Ralph's?'

'Christopher Weston. I knew him for quite a time . . .'

'Why not move nearer the front then . . .?'

'O this will be fine, thank you. You'll be a nephew?'

'John Thompson . . .'

'Ah, Ralph spoke of you. He worried about you at one time . . .'

'Can't think why. You must tell me more. Excuse me now, will you?' John dashed to guide three stringy cousins of Ralph who were insistently pushing their way into the second row. Once there, they ignored each other as they had for a year – since the last funeral.

And then the hired cars were at the gate. Pall bearers eased the coffin from its bower of late summer blossoms. The second car was crammed with wreaths. The third had no ornament but Ella.

When the choir, the curate and the coffin were settled, she walked alone up the aisle and remained at a prayer stool between the transepts. It is foolish to suppose that he who seizes the upstage

27

position grabs the audience. Ralph's coffin, glanced at as it passed, stood unnoticed. It was on Ella that attention, if not sympathy, focussed. Which leading actress would not have envied that cartwheel hat of raven's feathers, that veil of tulle drifting to the knees and the lavish cloak of charcoal watered silk that slurped along the marble aisle two yards behind the widow? Even to the unsympathetic, the huge chilled spray of orchids that she carried was a source of wonder. Was there not a month's supply of bread for some Indian village cupped in those plump hands?

The funeral service was much as any other though the Ladies' Guild did manage to adapt the Twenty Third Psalm to something strangely reminiscent of the Grand March from Aida. When the coffin was hoisted from its tressle during the closing hymn, attention was momentarily diverted from Ella. John noticed only a flash of watered silk from a side door as she drifted to her waiting car.

The congregation saw nothing of her at the rain-sodden graveside. She welcomed them all at the festively decorated dining room of the Simscombe Bay Hotel where she had not been idle.

Having won a little skirmish with the management on the seating plan, she'd rearranged the table decorations, shuffled the nametags of those who would be joining her on the raised dais and, so a cheeky waiter alleged in the kitchen, downed three double gins. Certainly she seemed newly fortified in her hour of anguish as she toured from group to group rehearsing the last hours of Ralph's illness and her own exhaustion. 'No one could say I disliked the man,' she conceded, 'I did put up with him for thirty five years. Not that you could guess just what I did have to put up with. I will admit, in a way, I'm glad he's gone.'

Now Vi, Ed's wife, was pregnant for the third time. That can be the only explanation for her indelicate behaviour at the top table. She, a mere niece by marriage, lobbied Ella twice in ten minutes about Ralph's Will.

'He left ten pounds,' snapped the widow in a tone that convinced all listeners that the information wouldn't be repeated. 'Which means I've paid for all this just as I've paid for every damn thing for years.'

'But what about that win of his at the races last season?' Vi persisted. And he was Works Manager. Surely there was a pension?' Poor girl, she feared any legacy was ebbing with the tide.

'Ralph was a fritterer like the rest of his family, Violet. Naturally he insisted that I took that world cruise after my prolapse. The least he could have done. Who caused it if he didn't? Mind you I made it clear from the day we were married that I wasn't interested in bedroom games. Twice he forced me and my prolapse was the result. Since you are so interested Violet I may as well tell you there was no Will. Everything comes to me. It is, if I may say so, most uncalled for on your part to talk of money on a day like this. I may find one or two keepsakes for you all.'

John would like to have talked to someone about his uncle but the Pension Fund representatives had left for London and the man in the grey suit, Christopher Weston, had not shown up. The three stringy cousins grinned encouragingly from behind a mound of ham sandwiches. No more cousins and no more ham sandwiches he shuddered and took his drink and a slice of cake into the sunlight waiting for the hotel booking to expire and for relatives to go back to *Dunromin*.

It would be his last look at a house for which he had never cared. Nothing of Ralph remained there. With his uncle's death, John was aware of a loss he'd been too young to comprehend when his own parents had been killed in their car. It had been Ralph's visits to various schools and hostels, seldom accompanied by Ella,that had brought some glitter and humour to the drabness of his adolescence.

Dunromin was, as it had always been, Ella's territory. John glanced into the lounge where tea was being sipped in silence. He searched for his aunt to offer excuses for leaving early. Guided by the rasp of her endless chatter, he went upstairs.

She was indeed dispensing keepsakes but he had the sense of disturbing something as he stood in a bedroom doorway. Four women were in the room. Was the prolapse under discussion again, John wondered? The speed with which Ella thrust a gold pencil at him confirmed his notion that he was an intruder.

'Something to remember your uncle by.' She was slightly drunk and very dismissive. 'A farewell gift from the factory, I believe. You'll have pawned it by the weekend no doubt. Feckless like the rest of them.' John's impulse was to thrust the gift into Ella's rat-trap mouth but Vi pulled her aside.

'Go on then Aunt Ella. Don't leave us up in the air. Is there proof?'

'You might have waited Violet. Not that it matters now. John might as well hear the truth.'

'Don't tell me he was pushing pot backstage at the Ladies' Guild, Aunt?'

'That I shall ignore with the contempt it deserves. I found some letters, I was telling them, when I turned out Ralph's things for jumble.'

'Blackmail were they?'

'Don't be sarcastic John. Let Aunt Ella finish.'

'Thank you Violet. In an old brown envelope they were, marked Gardening Hints.'

John, torn between interest and contempt, lit a cigarette.

'So, what were they? Tips for home poisoners?'

Ella produced a wisp of lace from her cuff. She dabbed her neck for the late afternoon was hot and trying.

'If you could stop being witty for just one second, John, you might begin to imagine how it feels to have lived with someone for years only to find he's been carrying on elsewhere most of the time.'

John choked on his cigarette smoke. Had he been anyone else Ella would have suspected he was weeping with sympathy. Had she been anyone else he might have done and had Ralph been anyone else he would have suspected such a situation long since as the only guarantee of sanity.

'So sorry,' he coughed, 'do tell more.'

'Some little London tart. No you're not going to read them. But I will show you a signature so there's no doubt in your minds. Here. "Ever yours, Chris". I always thought Christine a cheap little name.'

But what, thought John, if Chris were not Christine but

Christopher? The man in the back row . . . Christopher Weston? Aware of clumsy Vi burbling that since Ella had only just discovered the letters she'd hardly had to put up with much, John turned aside and realised he was rotating the gold pencil. There was no intertwined monogram R & C. That would have been too obvious yet he was certain, just as if he had been told, that the pencil was a retirement gift from Christopher Weston not from the factory. Betting that the man had arrived by train, John couldn't wait to leave for the station. Ella was smoothing the panels of her skirt. John recalled enough of her mannerisms to guess that the topic was closed and the subject was about to change.

'You're a fool Violet,' Ella was saying with elaborate articulation, 'There's a callousness about all your generation I shall never understand. Find me a drink John . . . and John,' she called as he was half down the stairs, 'what size shoes do you take?'

John did not hear the question the first time for he was wondering how Ralph had managed the deception for so many years. Mere chance, he chuckled to himself, that uncle and nephew had not collided now and again. Not that it would have mattered. Ella's voice broke in 'I said, "What size shoes do you take?"'

'Mine? Odd. I mean my feet are different sizes.' Incoherence covered horror. 'I have them specially built . . . that is, made. Very tiresome on my salary. Reminds me. I have to go. Now. Will someone in there pour a gin for Ella and take it up? I'll ring you Aunt,' he called, 'before you go on your jaunt. Sorry – recuperative cruise. Thanks for the pencil. It couldn't have gone to anyone better.'

Except to the rightful owner he added to himself, closing the garden gate. Ella stood in the porch, a large gin in her left hand and a pair of Ralph's brogues in her right.

He sprinted to the station, vaulted the barrier but a train was slowly pulling out on the up line. In the last compartment, his back to the engine, Christopher Weston was taking a last look at Simscombe. John stood waving the gold pencil like a frenzied hypnotist. The man noticed him at last, smiled then, seeing the pencil, moved his hand gently in a gesture that was half 'you keep it' and half 'goodbye'.

BUTTERFLIES

Until St Elred's won the Soccer Cup who'd even heard of the place? For one brief season its reputation glittered like a comet and was as quickly forgotten. Without Russ Green it's doubtful whether there would have been even that instant of glory. Not that he was the team captain or the goalie or even the bloke who sliced the lemons at half-time. He wasn't actually present to cheer the sweating eleven as they paraded before a grinning Minister of Education. Yet without Russ, that team of Student Teachers wouldn't have made it further than a preliminary knockabout against the local Chamber of Commerce.

Like too many of the students who had preceded them, the soccer team had had most of the stuffing knocked out of them before they enrolled to endure the St Elred's regime. The majority came to that tatty Victorian building well-drilled and apathetic from the surrounding sour industrial valleys. Consequently the constraints of the place did not appal them. There was chapel morning and night and no breakfast on Sundays until the orthodox had finished their eucharistic snack. There were three roll-calls a day to ensure that no one had defected. Hostel lights were switched off at ten thirty sharp. Any student found in a bar was sent down. All this, the tutors with their third class degrees and twelfth rate personalities managed to convince successive generations of eighteen year olds, was the proper climate in which our future teachers could flower as exciting human beings. All, that is, except Russ Green.

He'd returned to England from South Australia. Maybe Adelaide is not the globe's most cultured spot after say Salzburg or the Paris Left Bank but it is healthy. It does offer some space in the sun for teenagers to extend themselves. With fifteen sunny years behind him, even the bizarre restrictions of St Eldred's couldn't stunt Russ. They thwarted him to a fury. It was only through his incurable impulsiveness that he was there at all. Having decided to become a teacher – well, anyway, take the course – he discovered only St Elred's had spare places for the autumn term. It usually did. Less than a week after unpacking he could accept only one argument that he should remain another hour. Men. Three lovely hundred of them.

Not that he was seeking the ideal friend. Russ had no interest in damp meaningful walks through the surrounding farmlands. He just wanted men and plenty of them. If he had been accused of immorality, his reply would have been to point at the trim bodies around him dreaming of affection and twitching with inhibitions. His early overtures that first term led nowhere. One possible candidate suggested they should forget unhealthy talk and take a therapeutic dip in the icy river. Another clasped Russ by the shoulders (at last, at last, he thought) only to propose a joint prayer session. It was, Russ decided, as though the students had been trapped in a time warp that matched the grotesque architecture and the rules. Frustrating weeks dragged into months until – one March evening – Russ, trudging through the hostel grounds, spotted Cemlyn perched in the open window of a study not ten doors from his own. His curls were bright as new-hacked coal, his face freckled and his eyes mirrored the first decent sky for weeks. He was rolling a cigarette and listening to some sad orchestral piece. Russ sighed. The English take their pleasures strangely he thought as he developed an intense interest in some sooty daffodils that were struggling at Cemlyn's feet.

'You, matie,' he decided, 'are for me though you may not know it. I'll have you before the week's out.'

Before the evening was out as it happened. Since Cemlyn had never been with a man, Dutch courage was supplied through tots of brandy that Russ kept by him in a bottle labelled Cough Mixture. It was hoped that this would mellow Cemlyn sufficiently to recall that he did – despite all St Elred's conditioning – exist between the neck and the knees. After each of them had downed a third swig Russ uncurled on Cemlyn's bed – though they should by then have been in separate rooms studying the theory of Greek education. Two more brandies and Russ – commenting on the warmth of the evening – stripped, bronze and sturdy, to his briefs. Shadows from the setting sun obscured his mild acne and Cemlyn's blushes. One further tot in the toothglass and Cemlyn was nuzzling, eager but slightly aimlessly, on his visitor's chest.

Not that they completed the sexual alphabet that evening. Little more than a mild a, b, c for a start. Even so, they'd no sooner dabbed themselves on Cemlyn's flannel pyjamas than Russ was dampened for a second time.

'Will you ever speak to me again?' sobbed Cemlyn, 'My hand was tempted and I made the first move.'

Russ felt there was little point in replying, 'But I'd fucked you five times mentally before you'd even loosened your tie.' Instead he said, 'Think nothing of it.'

'But Russ, shall I ever be able to play centre-forward again?'

Ross slurped the last of the brandy down Cemlyn's eager throat.

'Didn't you know bull-fighters always have it beforehand to steady their glance? You'll do better than ever tomorrow. If you do score, private congratulations here at midnight might be in order.'

Cemlyn stared and began to splutter. Russ raised both eyebrows quizzically.

'Fretting about the prefects are you? Leave them to me. Don't ask and you can't tell. Save your energy for the game mate. Well, leave perhaps just a little over for later, eh?'

Russ himself wasn't certain how he'd outwit the college vigilantes. Prefects, he fumed as he whistled along to his own study, prefects. The place was a bloody prison hulk. They sleuthed through the dark in socks seeking chinks of light under doors, eager for evidence of illicit card schools or the clink of bottles. The real turds hoped for a whiff of scent from a smuggled barmaid or nurse.

Fortunately, he chuckled, the name, let alone, the interests, of Oscar Wilde would be unknown to them. Cemlyn did score – twice – and the team was set for the area quarter-finals. Such exuberance, everyone felt, almost indicated that Cemlyn was expecting some personal reward after the final whistle. Cemlyn blushed but said nothing. At supper he smiled discretely when Russ looked at him. The reply was a leisurely, meaningful wink.

About five to twelve that night Russ dragged on his dressing gown and paced silently along the corridor. He'd devised a plan that must outwit the prefects. Just as well for, having counted the doorways to Cemlyn's room carefully, he was disturbed by a torchbeam slicing the darkness on some stairs to his left. Russ felt rapidly for the next doorknob and crept inside.

When the torchlight had passed under the door he waited a moment and whispered, 'It's me.'

'Mmmm . . .'

'Coast's clear,' Russ muttered, shedding the dressing gown and sliding into the narrow bed. 'Relax,' he murmured, 'what's all this rigor mortis bit? A cuddle on a frosty night never harmed anyone yet,' and he began to caress the rigid pectorals next to him. Sensing some relaxation at last he felt gently down and then hesitated, quite perplexed. Russ had no penis fixation: to him piccolo or bassoon were equally pleasing yet he was sure his memory couldn't be faulty. The previous evening's sunset had plainly shown Cemlyn to be circumcised. In twenty-eight hours he'd regained a foreskin.

'Sure you're enjoying this?' he ventured.

'Mmmm,' was the only response. With a shrug Russ continued to explore. Whoever it was – and plainly it was not Cemlyn – began to reciprocate. By the time the chapel clock was striking two Russ was quite drained. He disengaged one hand to draw the curtain. The team goalie squinted at him in the moonlight then laughed softly.

'Knew it was you Russ. You've got fingers like the bloody butterflies painted on your wall.'

'Butterflies? It was you mate trembling like a Small Apollo. And

36

they come from black hairy caterpillars.'

'Don't get personal. Bugger it Russ, bet my game's ruined by all this.'

Russ assured him the folk-tales were nonsense and that he'd be brimming with phosphates long before he had to slip on his goalie's gloves again. At the weekend the goalie played a masterly game saving even the most sneaky of shots. Russ, on the touchline, observed not only his form but that of one or two other members of the team as well. He wasn't greedy and he knew his limitations but what greater community service could he offer than to ensure that St Elred's team kicked to victory assured and self-confident?

'Our right-back worries me Russ,' the goalie observed a few evenings later as they trooped in for compulsory hymn singing, 'needs to be told that he's a good performer – on the field, I mean.'

'What else could you mean?' whispered Russ archly.

Three hundred voices were yelling more or less in unison as a note was scribbled in the flyleaf of a hymnal suggesting a training jog as far as the haylofts overlooking the estuary. Russ ripped out the sheet and sent it along the row to the half-back who read it and smiled appreciatively. A lad of few words, he smiled just as appreciatively the following evening as he and Russ pulled wisps of straw from each other's pubic hair.

The Cup Final for Student Teacher's Colleges attracted wide attention. League team managers announced that they would be present. And then, the night before, Russ and Cemlyn simultaneously had one hideous thought. They were lolling on a mattress in the moonlit gym.

'What,' said Cemlyn voicing it for both, 'if one of us is injured?'

Russ tapped the Cough Mixture bottle solemnly as they considered the first reserve: a sniffy youth with symptoms of ingrown virginity.

'Snape wouldn't let us down,' Russ asserted, glancing at his watch and yawning.

'Wish I shared your confidence. He's unpredictable, that's what he is. Eaten out with jealousy. Reckons we're all whoring and boozing while he trains. Too bloody virtuous by half is Snape.'

'Probably he's into sweaty socks and smelly wellies. Come on. Bedtime. By yourself.'

As Cemlyn slept with a contented smile, Russ drifted through the quiet corridor to Snape's room.

Like the rest it was heavily curtained so only the breathing could guide him. He stroked the sleeper's forehead gently. The breathing became turbulent. He touched the neck. The breathing became a gurgle. He played a little light music on Snape's left nipple. It hardened instantly. Russ, overjoyed that the game was saved whatever happened, dropped onto the bed and slid his left hand under a sweating neck. There was less than three second silence before Snape, louder than any Town Crier, screamed, 'Rape . . . Murder . . . Help.'

Russ jack-knifed to his feet. Corridor lights were being switched on. Doors were opening. Time, he decided, to operate the Emergency Plan.

Spreading both arms before him and thinking of Lady Macbeth he strolled naked into the corridor and made for his room. Students and tutors converging on Snape's screams glanced of course but – noting Russ's unblinking stare – did not intercept him. Alone in his study Russ guessed – accurately – that he'd be undisturbed until morning and then the drama would begin.

The Venerable Principal arrived before breakfast carrying an abandoned dressing gown. While Russ shaved, his visitor studied the flight of butterflies that ornamented one wall. Russ developed a colourful explanation for his sleepwalking. The Principal continued to stare at the butterflies.

'Green,' he pouted finally, 'were you attempting to sodomise Snape?'

'Venerable Principal, I've already told you. The whole thing is a blank. As I said, there was an unfortunate occurrence during my Australian childhood. The beachguard who saved me from drowning used me to practice for his Advanced Kiss Of Life Certificate . . .'

'St Elred's men are a byword for honesty and unquestionable morality, Green. You should perhaps consider your future . . .' the watery glance swivelled to the wall once more. 'What have you in common with our Soccer Eleven? Don't vex me by suggesting that they share your passion for butterflies. I have doubts about you working with the young, Green. I have doubts.'

'You mean I'm out?'

'You're trembling on the doorstep,' snapped the Venerable Principal, wafting away to breakfast like a dizzy bat.

Russ told Cemlyn and Cemlyn told the team. At least six were aghast though in front of the rest they didn't show it.

On the Venerable Principal's desk an hour later were five scribbled notes delivered when each writer was certain he'd not been observed. The team captain, having the leadership qualities that go with the job, demanded an interview.

'Are you hinting,' hissed the Principal, gripping his Prayer Book like a talisman, 'that you and other members of our team have been having unspeakable relations with Russ Green.'

'That's about it, Principal. I've slept with him. I can't answer for the others but I can say: if Russ goes, we go sick. Then it's no game; no victory; no Cup. No congratulations from the Minister afterwards of course and, I suppose, no Honours List for you.'

'Am I to connive at filling the classrooms of the future with the depraved?'

'Would you prefer to fill the papers with scandal? Look, Principal, Russ has shown me affection, see? Now while you've been mugging up all the theory in that book of yours, we've been getting on with it like.'

'This conversation did not take place. Green may stay – for the moment. He may not watch the match and may most certainly not meet the Minister.'

Of course St Elred's won, fortunately without injuries since Snape was resting under sedation. Later that first warm April evening the Minister and the Venerable Principal wandered through the hostel gardens.

'Was that a champagne cork popping?'

'Hardly Minister, our lads don't imbibe. Just the innocent sounds of table tennis.'

'Pity,' grunted Her Majesty's Secretary of State.

'The trout pond's this way,' urged the Principal shuffling nervously from the hostel walls.

'Can't drink bloody pond-water,' moaned the Minister, 'could do with a snort.'

'I could offer you a glass of cider,' panted the Principal tottering at some speed to stand firmly on a pair of ornamented soccer shorts that had floated from a ground floor window. He placed one unfeeling foot on each of the flimsy butterfly transfers when two voices, both drunk and one recognisably Australian, began to sing Mozart's Alleluia enthusiastically but slightly off-key, the Principal fluttered his hands and beamed at the Minister.

'As you can hear, we at St Elred's have our minds on higher things,' he said.

TELL ONE PERSON ONLY

Since you have undertaken such a journey the least I could offer was half my meal. No more than a hundred days on the road? That was swift. For six full months my fingers froze as I had to slink from hill farm to woodland settlement – simple households that kept to the old ways, you understand? Some evenings, looking across the bay here at great Hercules' rock I wonder if there is still money on my head in England after forty years. With grasping Henry dead, I hear from merchants in our market there has been war between cousins at home and yet . . . nothing calls me back.

You tell me you live quietly, covering your head and your heart like the old grey beggar at the crossroads? I, too, dreamed once that I might live by working my father's farms and hiding among the mutes at the back of churches when the monks demanded it. We spoke of that – he and I – one morning as we walked under the cherry trees watching sunbeams fondle the roof of his new hall by the river.

'Cedric,' he said softly – and, with me, he did not stutter, 'the hall will stand, as you will, for seasons after my death whichever summer that comes. When they question you, speak without guard on your tongue – add ornaments as our singers do. My name will be coal-black, that has been agreed. Adopt their ways, observe their doleful festivals and live at peace on your father's land.'

Perhaps because I smiled and had never spoken falsely to him he believed I would. At that moment – no more than fifteen months before I had to make the choice – I did dream of playing the fox with them.

Before the cherries were ripe he was riding from London to choke the rebels of the north. I, being alone, played my harp in the evenings so softly to myself that I could overhear the whispers. Like the waves of the Thames under the walls, their scheming never ended. All that they plotted, they would have been quick to say, was in the name of the Prince of Peace. It was they who planned the deaths of blithe young courtiers who laughed and danced so that they could seem accidents to us, yet be given out to the serfs as the anger of their god. Once, in a cellar, I stumbled on two of them whittling eyesockets in a statue that would weep small cups of water to amaze the simple. I knew them then, those priests who had sailed with the Conqueror. Just as he subdued England's anger so they journeyed about like robber barons to enslave men's spirits until it was no longer possible for the old ways to continue not overtroubled by the new. It was then I saw that to stay at home after his death, trying to cover my heart as a bird does her nest, would be useless. From that night on I perfected each step of my escape, planning exactly what I must do like the details of a battle. The only falsehood I ever practised was in not telling one word of it to Rufus.

On the edge of this fishing village, at last I am among people who do not try to make me what I am not. They do not even ask that I revere their local prophet. To them – and this may interest you – the Jewish carpenter's son is very respected – but as a man, like you, like me and their own chief prophet.

You are impatient. Will the old fool, you are whispering to yourself, tell me what he knew of the Red King? Maybe, my friend . . . but first, as those monks who grip our green land in their claws might say, I must put you to the test. No, no no . . . I see white spots of fear at the corners of your eyes. No fires for the good of your soul. We don't keep hot irons or casks of water to draw what we want to hear from you. Does their Prince of Peace tell them how to use such things? Forgive me, friend, it is not only the feet of old men that ramble. You, being young, are eager as a hound on the scent but – to me – little is urgent. Now . . . to our test. You have no ink or parchment with you? O, you are right, such objects might have made men suspicious of any wayfarer. No matter, I keep both to hand. So. We will discover if your pen is as swift and sure as an arrow. Forgive me if I close my eyes. Happenings so long ago dance less wantonly in the darkness. Write this then young traveller . . .

My father, Adelbert, was a prosperous Saxon – an Earl with farms that opened like a fan to the west of the new forest the Conqueror planted – that great boneyard watered with Saxon blood and tears. Being lame, my father did not follow Harold, our last gold warrior to the northern war and then to his death in Kent. We sent food and beer from home for the bowmen until, with the Conqueror made king, we knew the greasy Normans would not leave. My father withdrew to his hearthside, paid his taxes and we worked the fields. It is from his family – which I favour in many ways – that my colouring comes. Rufus would say my glance was like the flash of kingfisher's wings. An old soldier, wounded at Hastings, picked me up from my willow cradle and joked with my mother that my red cheeks were borrowed from the clay slopes that rose beyond our stream. By the September day that Rufus himself was crowned I could use the Norman tongue as nimbly as my own. My mother, shrewd woman, overruled my father in that.

'When Cedric is a man,' she would say, 'there will not be two peoples in one land.'

He listened to her as we all did for she could tell her family back to priests of Odin. Her words rang true, though she did not foresee how my friendship with the king would fulfil them.

On the night of the holy harvest dances in that same year when Rufus was crowned at Westminster, while new cider strong with iron horseshoes went the rounds and grey monks beyond the millrace heard with horror our old songs that did battle with their chanting, a great storm broke. No doubt the monks cackled that it was a judgement on us. Surely it was a portent for me. We had gone, I can still see it clearly, into the hall and were bolting the shutters when the king and his knights, losing their path on the road to Exeter, took refuge. I was by then, you know, twenty years of age: as skilled in music as in horsemanship. Father, hoping I might be sure enough of the Norman's favour to be free to inherit our lands or even – our family's dream – be allowed to use our title again other than in whispers, pushed me forward to play for the guests as they ate.

Shy of the foreigners, torn two-ways by fear of a king and anger at what his family had already done (how many Earls' ladies were dairy-women on their own farms and their lords strung up in Salisbury town?) I played to them but would not sing. Nor did I look up once, not even as I strummed the old harp to silence when, under my brows, I watched the apples and brambleberries and cheeses carried in and set on the board.

It was then, in a silence, that I first heard him speak. 'Encore . . . Br-bravo . . .' shouted the thick voice. So I looked at Rufus the red-faced, noting the spun-gold hair, the clean-shaven chin and the grey eyes. Could he, I wondered, be kinsman to the strangers we had glimpsed, dark and lean as axes, galloping through our villages and our crops and hens as proud as emperors?

'Now a s-song . . . a S-saxon one . . . a b-ballad with thirteen verses,' he growled. I looked towards my mother and saw amazement in her stare. There's little need to tell you, friend, that thirteen was the password inviting me to tell some chronicle of the year, sacred to our outlawed religion. Was it some trap or was this new king a man who secretly followed the left-hand path? I sang him the song of the trees in their seasons. It is like a nut covered in honey, my mother would say, for only those with the teeth of knowledge could taste the inner meaning. As I sang I studied the king and I knew that he had tasted and liked that inner meaning. Yet as I looked at him I trembled for he was appraising me in a way no being had ever done – not my parents, nor the village girls. It was not, you must write, the hungry stare I saw in a young monk's eyes as he corrected my French. One of the knights, watching Rufus, murmured to another and they began to chuckle. With the back of his fist the king clouted both their heads while never taking his glance from me. I knew I was being offered friendship as surely as if he had held out his open hand. And something more, something rare to which I could not put a name, beyond the friendship of the hunt and the drinking bowl . . .

That, friend, is something we also need just now to refresh ourselves. Let me see if you have kept pace with the darting swallow of my words. But your page is still blank as milk . . . have I been wasting the afternoon? You did not tell me you could not use a pen. Each word locked fast in your head? We'll test if there is some trick soon enough. How did I begin? Come now, the very words . . . so . . . good . . . very good. The old skills then are not buried and forgotten in England?

What test, friend? O but you have passed. That was the test. Can you think I would have trusted you with one true word to take back if you had been able to write it down? A parchment, in cunning hands, could be copied but altered in the copying . . . a word carefully lost here and a damning phrase slid in like a spy there. Have no doubt, my words would have been stolen from you, wherever you hid them, as evidence for their other lies. A king's friendship would have been cheapened from gold to dross to frighten the young and to pleasure the monkish writers as they conjured turds and venom from their own depths.

It has all happened as Rufus warned me. You and I can do nothing to sweeten the brutish face of him they will hand on but then we, too, have our way, yes? We can pass from lip to ear the story of a man whose kinsmen were the lion, the oak and the sun in its high splendour.

My friend, we are ignoring the customs of a country that has been civil enough to house me without question. Here, in the afternoons we rest. Through there you will find another couch. You will have noticed as we ate that these serving boys are un- skilled in our northern tongues. There are some languages without borders however . . . these they know . . . unless you wish to rest, perfecting all that I have told you so far?

So be it. This evening we will walk slowly – it is the habit here – and look across the water to the fires of Europe. Old trees burning; old men buring, too, who will not renounce the ancient ways. Later, when we have had supper, I will tell you something of Rufus and the old festivals. He was truly a blood-brother to the sun and knew from his birth that one summer, in a beggarly harvest, he would die to nourish the soil though he would not have guessed it would be in England. No, he was not murdered by his whoring brother Henry. I saw the death from the shadow of the elder trees. I did not weep until I was a day's gallop from the spot, riding west to the islands beyond Cornwall. There, with a little of the gold he often gave me, I was blown with the fishermen to France. Enough of that. I shall not say more of his death . . . that will often be spoken of. You must know more of his life with me, almost thirteen full years of friendship. Forget all the lies you must have heard of a court with more bestial couplings daily than Roman Caligula could ever dream of. It is true that Rufus had handsome young knights about him. He delighted in the company of those who enjoyed this one life of which we can be sure. The whey-faced monks he would keep waiting at the doors in all weather.

'Let them look up,' he would smile, 'there'll be a clear sky soon and then they can choose their own particular perches on the clouds.'

His courtiers were handsome and amusing but the friendship of his bed was mine. 'Let's celebrate two peoples made one,' he'd whisper when he tired of a banquet or with long hours of giving judgement without favour to high and low.

Once an Archbishop overheard his invitation to me and tightened his lips like a purse. 'Your Grace,' Rufus said with a solemn face, 'I was suggesting to the friend of my bosom that we should go to a more private place. There I call him John and he calls me . . .' the Archbishop went purple as his cloak with anger, '. . . and he calls me, your Grace, Rufus as I'm sure you are kind enough to do behind my back.'

Rufus, though he could neither read nor write, was never bested by a monk. What is this new foolishness that leads men to suppose only those who can use a pen have wit?

I must rest, friend, and you must recall each phrase. When you are in England again let no man write it down. Tell one person only, the friend you can trust – the one with whom you lie secretly on the eve of the great May festival in the greenwoods. When you are sure of him, recount to him softly the story of Rufus and Cedric. Who can say if an evening will close in when such a story can be told at the open hearth? It will not be from your mouth or that of your friend's young friend not yet born. None of that is important to me. It is sufficient that I loved a man and was loved. Yes; it was only Rufus. We should not ask for such joy twice.

THE SKATERS

'Funny time to be doing the place up,' Mr Cunliffe gasped as he squatted on a cabin trunk.

Stan didn't reply until he'd commuted once more into the bedroom and returned with two suits on their hangers. Having smoothed them deftly into a case, he remarked to the room in general, 'In the lease, see? Leave everything as we found it. We both signed.'

Mr Cunliffe sighed and relit his pipe.

'Let us have an address Stan. We might just hear something. His mother still has hopes.'

'Sorry I can't make you a cup of tea,' Stan said, concentrating on the ties he was folding. 'Write *poste restante*, York . . . . if anything turns up like.'

'D'you know you've been living with this carpet the wrong way up? A couple of lads wouldn't spot that, of course.' With the stem of his pipe the old man pointed at a frayed criss-cross of threads. 'You'd think they'd let tenants have something a bit more classy – considering the price they were asking.'

'Fact is,' Stan gulped as he bounced on a case so that the lock would fasten, 'I went a bit heavy with the old emulsion like. Looks like a snowdrift the right side up. Won't tumble to it straight off though, will they?'

Mr Cunliffe seemed no longer interested.

'His mother's still in a state you know.' He shook his head and addressed a collection of carrier-bags in the middle of the floor.

'Before I came round, I said to her "Mother, if our Barrie's in trouble he'll contact his parents. He always did". She's of a different mind though. Reckons he would come to you.'

'Waited a fortnight, didn't I?' Stan observed, reopening an overnight bag to cram in his sponge-bag. 'Couldn't carry on with this rent solo, see?'

Having surveyed the denuded flat and the luggage yet again Mr Cunliffe shook his head two or three times and sniffed. He took his pipe from his mouth and cleared his throat. Not looking up he spoke slowly; flatly.

'No offence eh, Stan? I mean that. No offence like . . . there wasn't anything well . . . wrong between you and our Barrie was there?'

Looking the older man in the eye when he finally glanced up, Stan laughed.

'What should there have been then?' he said quickly. 'Never rowed did we? Me, I'm as stunned as you are Mr Cunliffe. Flattened I am, straight. Know no more than you do. Barrie went off to a party and never came back. Finish. Borrowed two quid come to think of it. Had to buy a present.'

'That wasn't exactly what I was on about Stan . . .'

'You astound me Mr Cunliffe. What was you on about then? Go on, let's have it . . . what's eating you?'

'Forget it. No, no . . . forget it, son. Hell of a lot of gear you've got to shift here. What's all those little parcels on the deck there?'

'Those are Easter eggs Mr Cunliffe. The Kanes are a far-flung family.'

Stan went through to the kitchen to find matches for himself as Mr Cunliffe relit his pipe.

'Mrs Cunliffe says you're one of the quiet ones. She means never letting on about any young ladies. Looks like she's right again. Usually hits things on the head does Mother.'

He looked up to find Stan smiling in the kitchen doorway, an unlit cigarette in his hand.

'Barrie's bits are in the carriers Mr Cunliffe. I'd have brought them round on me way. Wasn't expecting you to call really. Only

50

Barrie's Mum ever came before. Funny way for us to get acquainted this, you might say.'

Mr Cunliffe nodded, not so much at Stan's words as at the elastic bandage on his wrist.

'Hurt yourself then?' he asked.

'That? Nothing. Nothing at all. Bit of a strain that's all. Had to drag all these boxes on me own, see? Could have done with a hand from Barrie I must admit.'

'What about his skates Stan?'

The question had to be repeated for Stan had disappeared back into the kitchen and was, from the sound of it, washing his hands vigorously.

'Barrie was my mate Mr Cunliffe,' he replied slowly drying his hands with some thoroughness on a clean handkerchief. 'Mind if I keep them? That might seem soft to those of a callous nature but . . . I'd like to. Never know, eh? Might hear from him any day now.'

'Sheila was round last night. She thinks we should inform the Police. She's very concerned, is Sheila.'

'What the hell's it to her?'

Stan dropped the sodden handkerchief, retrieved it with an angry dash of his hand and thrust it in his pocket.

'Well, it was her party. Mrs Cunliffe has kept on ever since about how she wishes you'd gone too. I mean, you could have kept an eye on Barrie . . . Don't you care for Sheila, Stan?'

'It's not a case of liking or disliking. I felt sick. Barrie was in two minds about going, with me being under the weather. "Suit yourself" I said. My exact words. "Go if you want to" I said "I'm staying put." I could feel one of my heads coming on if you want the truth Mr Cunliffe.'

'Sheila's most upset. She let on to Barrie's Mum that they'd come to an understanding that night on the patio. Only natural that Sheila should feel involved.'

'Stupid possessive cow. Always was. Phoning here regular as clockwork if we was so much as ten minutes late at the Rink. Barrie hated being hassled – now you know that without me telling you.

Know what I think Mr C? I reckon Barrie's split for a month or so. Needs some peace from Sheila-interfering-Noakes.'

'You could be right Stan. I was like him meself at his age. Time he settled down though, you must agree. In his twenty sixth year now. Can't laugh your way through life shirking responsibilities, can you son? Shall I give you a hand down to the car?'

Mr Cunliffe gathered some carrier-bags. Two contained his son's clothes. Another was heavier with saws, hammers and chisels.

'Like to see a man keep the tools of his trade in good nick,' he gasped as he examined the oiled blades and well-scrubbed shafts.

Ten minutes later they had ferried most of the portable luggage to the back seat of Stan's estate-wagon. On their final journey they stumbled down balancing the cabin trunk between them.

'Gawd Almighty, boy, got half the Borough Library in here have you?' Mr Cunliffe panted as they heaved and shoved it into the boot.

'I have what's called an acquisitive nature Mr Cunliffe. Can't bear to be parted from anything I take a fancy to,' smiled Stan, brushing dust from his suit. 'Hang about now. I'll nip back and lock up. I can drop you off and sling the keys in the agent's on my way. No sweat.'

When Mr Cunliffe protested that he lived on the far side of town and would be holding things up, Stan shrugged.

'Suit yourself,' he said and ran up the stone steps whistling.

As he disappeared round the turn of the stairs Mr Cunliffe counted up to three and whisked one of the carrier-bags from the passenger seat. The blades of Barrie's skates protruded from the fancy gift paper in which each had been neatly wrapped. One, he decided, could go to Sheila and the other could hang in the hall beside the barometer. He was easing the carrier under an over-grown privet with his heel as Stan returned.

'Forgot something you might like to have Mr Cunliffe,' Stan smiled as he unlocked the cabin trunk and fumbled among books, papers, bats and trophies. 'There we are then . . . see? . . . Me and Barrie enjoying ourselves.'

The colour-snap was of two young men, fresh from swimming, their arms round each others' waists. The background was a calm sea and an island blurred by heat-haze.

'That's nice Stan. Very thoughtful. His mother will treasure that . . . you don't think he got Sheila pregnant do you? Skidaddled because he couldn't face the music, so to speak?'

'Barrie would've come to me see? We had no secrets Mr C. We was inseparable. Peas in a pod. Shared everything, understand? Everything . . . Right then, see you around Mr Cunliffe.'

Stan drove to the end of the avenue, doubled back through the side streets and made for the coast road and the Continental Ferry.

Mr Cunliffe, slowed a little by the carrier-bags, trudged among the home going crowds. He left one skate, with a note, on Sheila's doorstep and then plodded on to his own terraced house. His wife had already set their tea things on the table.

'Well Mother,' he said, warming his calves at the electric fire, 'no news really. He's a quiet one, that Stan, just like you said. D'you know, it wouldn't amaze me if he was off this very minute to some assignation with a lady friend.'

'This all we've got then to remind us of our Barrie?' Mrs Cunliffe complained, fingering a couple of pairs of jeans and a tartan shirt or two.

'Now that's where you're wrong. Just between ourselves I was crafty for once. Justified though, Mother. Nothing on my conscience. Can you beat it? That Stan was going to scarper with our lad's skates. I wasn't having that, was I?'

'So where are they?'

'I left one for Sheila on my way home. Something for her to remember him by eh? Now this one would go nicely in the passage, I reckoned.'

'I shall always see him doing one of those fancy twirls of his every time I pass it,' Mrs Cunliffe sniffed, extracting the boot from its wrapping. 'Nice new laces, too . . .'

'Always attentive to little details was Barrie,' observed her husband, filling his teacup.

'Fetch over my glasses will you?' Mrs Cunliffe, puzzled, was

53

dangling the boot as she spoke. 'My, this does seem heavy.'

She did not need glasses, however, to identify Barrie's left foot, sawn at the ankle and tightly bandaged. Fascinated, they watched it slide into the semolina pudding.

A REMARKABLY CIVILISED ARRANGEMENT

One colleague – a Freudian through and through – dismissed Ewan as anally retentive about money but then, as Ewan said, it was an opinion based on limited observation in the Common Room. It is true that for those forty weeks of the year he spent in Britain – or so he admitted to me – Ewan never, ever entertained at his apartment. Some supposed he had a distaste for strangers fingering his possessions. The Freudian psychologist, Ewan had heard, improvised further and wondered if he might be among that curious few who, rather than have visitors use their bathrooms, provide a pile of coins by the street door with a handy sketch-map showing the nearest public conveniences.

The truth is that Ewan was neither mean nor a walking casebook of the rarer human quirks. Very coolly (for he was an engineer proud that he controlled his passions) the man had worked out his priorities. Why not? Money is never elastic. He would have agreed that during term he existed. In his own phrase: vacations were for living. Not entirely a recluse between Christmas and Easter, he emerged, so he alleged, from time to time at parties though he never took a bottle. 'Not drinking at the moment. Getting over a stomach bug,' he would murmur. He would ignore the waspish asides of 'Too bloody mean,' from others as inaccurate. In this he was correct for he allotted so much and no more for existence through the grey English winter: the balance of his disposable income he banked against his next voyage of discovery. Colleagues never even surmised where Ewan might have vanished in the drizzle as the final chords of 'Lord Dismiss Us

With Thy Blessing' rumbled round the college corridors. 'Too stingy,' they sneered – if what had been reported to him was true, 'to drift round to the local for a celebratory beer'. Since he never discussed his vacations with any of them in retrospect and pretended his tan had been poured from a bottle, how should fellow-lecturers have guessed, downing a third round, that Ewan was checking in at the airport for Amsterdam, Tangier, San Francisco or Hong Kong? And, if they had, few would have deduced a common factor from his destinations.

And so three times per annum, while others back home grumbled no doubt that teaching hours were all very fine but the salary allowed little more than existence during vacations, Ewan would be emerging from drab flannels and worn, elbow-patched jacket like some resplendent butterfly – his blue jeans carefully bleached and candy-striped shirt unbuttoned to his navel. Vacations were for living.

It's not possible to outline the pattern of Ewan's previous holidays or his impact on those he met around the gay capitals of our five continents for I wasn't about at the time. I met him in Tangier where I was sucking in the April sunshine and recuperating after a tiresome operation. Had that sunshine been undiluted, I doubt we would have met. I'd puffed my way as nippily as I could into a beach cafe to shelter from a sudden short-lived storm. Ewan had divined, though I'd ordered in French as colloquially as I could, that I might possibly be English. Had I hid my cigarettes less clumsily he might not have noticed the packet and then wondered with a smile if I, like himself, was a first-timer in Morocco. I was not.

Whether he had a history of selecting and then romanticising some Dutchman on Rembrandtplein, an Aussie at Kings Cross or winsome lads on Castro I couldn't know but, in Tangier, before my pot of coffee arrived from the kitchen he was extolling Omar. It was soon clear that Ewan was obsessed with him. Omar was no predatory beach boy. Educated at the High School he had, through his father's clerical job at a Consulate, been found a post with his country's Embassy in South Europe and was home on leave. Ewan had met him in a bar or rather Ewan had met a longed-for ideal who'd but the haziest resemblance to the rest of humankind that sweats, has needs, snores occasionally and also shits.

It was equally sad that Ewan had overlooked the commonplace that, in warmer climates, immediate needs seek immediate satisfaction. Our gloomy northern winters afford too much contemplation and brooding over goals. Undeniably the occasional genius is produced but Ewan McLeish was neither Sibelius nor Ibsen though he'd done his share of brooding. While the lightminded had frittered their youth and their capital at discos and glittering premieres, Ewan had considered the ideal relationship and had plundered the public library for almost all that's been written about the quest for one's Platonic other half. Each vacation he had flown north, west, east and now south in search of him.

Omar, I began to gather, was understandably bewildered. In Ewan I supposed he'd seen another tourist – no flibbertigibbet camping along the Boulevard Pasteur – but an intelligent being of passable appearance. Since both were on holiday all would seem to have been set for a pleasant three weeks. Unfortunately Omar was arguing, I was told, that they ought to share a pillow at night as well as afternoons on the beach and evenings in the bars.

While the storm was clearing Ewan explained that this debate had raged until two in the morning on five consecutive days. He, however, remained adamant: before consummation, one ought to be sure. Omar, he enthused, was worth much more than a quick fumble in a changing hut. Omar had refinement and a competence in English that might well fit him for a shared household in Britain once Ewan was certain they were truly matched.

'You can't get Tangerines to flourish on a headland by the North Sea' I warned, having watched that disaster too many times.

Not that Ewan listened for neither my reservations nor Omar's protests could come between the dreamer and his often-rehearsed fulfilment.

'We've plenty of time for all that,' he concluded as the sun came out. 'Now I insist you join us for a drink this evening.'

'Playing gooseberry isn't my bag. And I'm not doing my United

Nations Act to defuse these rows the two of you seem to be enjoying.'

'Do come,' Ewan repeated, 'I've a car booked for the morning and we're away to the south then for three whole days . . .'

'And nights . . .'

'Omar is an excellent driver.'

'Good to hear you'll let him do something for you,' I smiled as we wandered out onto the street where steam was rising from the stones.

'Right then, I'll be at the Tangerine Bar around ten . . . no more than an hour though. Early nights for me at the moment.'

Ewan waved and walked purposefully off towards the old town and the markets.

Omar certainly had distinction, was taller than the usual Moroccan and though clearly in his late twenties wasn't bloated from a sugar and carbohydrate diet. After a couple of minutes I'd also sussed he was not inexperienced in relationships with his own sex. Not that he gave me any reason to suppose he might be one of the sad beach pests eternally seeking a tourist who'd provide a work permit and a fare on the strength of a fresh and willing smile. Omar paid for a round of drinks immediately I walked in though perhaps they'd not reckoned on the glass door in which I'd seen reflected the hasty passing of a fistful of dirhams. What, I wondered, would those college critics who'd condemned Ewan for parsimony have thought of that?

We discussed farming in each other's countries and unemployment. Since they were both content to let me steer the conversation away from the personal I did have a hope that they'd resolved their problem. No sooner had Ewan wandered off to the loo than Omar became confidential.

'You are Ewan's friend . . .'

'Met him this morning . . .'

'But you are both from Britain. He would talk to you. What does he say is wrong with me?'

'Nothing adverse, take it from me. We all enjoy a bit of flattery but I'm not going to turn your head with all he's said about you.'

58

'Ewan is a gentleman. So are you. But something is very wrong. I want to go to bed with him but he won't let me. How am I unworthy of him? Please . . . I must know.'

I looked at the innocuous orange juice in my glass then lifted it to sniff the heavy lacing of Spanish brandy.

'Let's put it this way Omar. Ewan might be scared the experience wouldn't measure up to the – well – anticipation. You should tell him it's never really rainbows and trumpets the first time for any of us. The great trick is to work at it . . . to combine the high of the first time with the laid back approach that grows with trust.'

Ewan came back and we reverted to chatter about smuggling to and from Europe in the fishing boats. I did sense some relaxation in Omar though I could hardly credit it to anything I'd said. When he, too, went for a piss, Ewan couldn't wait for the swing door to close before tackling me.

'You realise I only walked out to the corner so that you could talk to him? I knew he'd listen to you. You'll agree he seems calmer already . . .'

'I'll agree he's less prone to squabble than I feared. I couldn't give him any answers Ewan. You two must sort it yourselves . . . Hold on. I'll pay – this must be the last round if you don't mind.'

They walked me back to my apartment block full of their trip to the south. I invited them in for coffee but Omar refused, saying that he had to cross the city to his mother's to pack a suitcase and get some sleep.

'Fine,' I said, glad that I could call it a day. 'When you're both back – with your little local difficulty solved – drop round for a drink. The concierge knows my comings and goings. Number forty five.'

The tinny bell of the Anglican church was clanging eleven as I watched them walk, not with that intimacy of lovers which bridges the space between them, down the steps towards the Boulevard d'Espagne. It was not, I sighed, the way in which two newly-rediscovered Platonic halves coherred.

Rather pleased that I'd not be slipping into a tiresome routine of morning coffee and a catalogue of the latest non-intimacies with Ewan each morning at the Cafe de Paris, I had a shower, turned off the light and paused a moment, looking over the bay. There was a shimmer of phosphorous on the tideless sea at the other extremity of which Greeks had once written so much that was now proving Ewan's undoing. I smiled, recalling an aunt who, amazed that I was unmarried at forty, remarked, 'Well, there's someone for everybody. It's just a case of matching up at the right time and place'. I'd not contradicted her nor even hinted that I'd long since accepted love and life in the variety of ways they are served up.

There was a soft knock at my door. The night porter, the wrinkled vestige of what might once have been the pick of the beach (had he known Gide? His father, maybe, chatted up from time to time by Wilde?) was grinning through what teeth remained and easing up his stained djellabah to offer a quivering erection.

'Too kind,' I muttered, 'in some other incarnation yet to come, maybe but . . . not tonight Abdul.'

I shut the door on him, bolted it and went to bed.

Five minutes later the tapping came again. Regardless of neighbours or whether they understood English I yelled, 'Piss off. Now.'

There was a brief respite then a muffled whisper.

'It's Omar.'

Maybe I shouldn't have been surprised. In a trice his need for satisfaction – to prove himself a darn sight better than the next man at a car wheel as it were – had been deflected from Ewan to me. To Omar, or so it seemed, any advice I'd given in the Tangerine had been less relevant than the opportunity it gave him to assess what he saw as pragmatic commonsense by comparison with Ewan's high ideals.

'Changed your mind about coffee then?' I asked, knowing the answer and knowing, too, he must be aware of the idle question since I was rebolting the door behind him.

He turned and, lacing his hands behind my neck, moved his head forward so that our foreheads touched. My own hands gripped his waist and I pulled our bodies together.

'Ewan wouldn't understand,' he said, running his nose down the bridge of my own, 'but I think you do. I want you very much.'

'I gathered that since your proud sex seems to be rearing itself at a healthy speed,' I laughed.

When we'd made love a second time Omar wanted to discuss Ewan, himself and me. I slid a cigarette into his mouth and yawned that too often people exhaust desire in chatter so we finished our cigarettes in silence, made love again and set the travelling-clock alarm for six forty.

By ten to seven Omar had showered and was whistling down the stairs on his way to grab his suitcase and apologise at Ewan's hotel for oversleeping. In odd moments, lying in the sun that day and the next, I thought of them touring Fez and Rabat and wondered how it might be going with them.

The morning following their return Ewan was at my door before I'd finished breakfast while Omar, as usual, helped his mother in the market.

'No need to ask if it went well,' I called, hunting for a clean coffee cup.

'Marvellously. Omar has seen the need for caution. You appear to have done wonders . . .'

'I have?' I dried a cup, artlessly playing for time. 'How so?'

'Omar's told me everything. How he came back here the other night (that took care of any hints from the rejected porter) and how you spent hours convincing him that impetuous lust is no foundation for a civilised relationship. When he did get home, he overslept you know . . .'

I scurried away from the quicksands.

'But the physical side is all right now between you?'

'That can come later,' Ewan smiled, stirring his coffee rhythmically, 'we shared a bed of course but Omar was quite satisfied with a goodnight kiss.'

Poor sod, I thought.

'Now are you going to join us again this evening?' Ewan was asking probably for the second time since I'd been recalling just how satisfying Omar had been in bed.

'Well, why not? And what about your hotel tomorrow morning for coffee eh? Just the two of us for a bit of a gossip?'

'That,' Ewan glowed, 'sounds a remarkably civilised arrangement.'

And so it was. For the next two weeks we drank in the Tangerine until I covered a yawn at ten thirty and then – at the last stroke of the Anglican church bell – Omar's stockinged feet padded along to my door.

When they saw me off at the airport Ewan said three times that he would write. He did but with my left hand I scrawled Gone Away: Address Unknown on each envelope and reposted them. Omar offered nothing more than a smile and I, distracting Ewan's glance for just a moment, mouthed him a kiss in return.

LOVE BITES

The ffordes would not have made the finals of the Radiant Honeymoon Couple of the Year Contest. Caroline perched on an extinct radiator in one corner of the Waiting Room, chain-smoking. Roy stared from a window opposite, willing the signal on the up-line to change from red to green. Neither had spoken for twenty minutes. The only sound was that of rain overflowing inadequate guttering above the platform.

The tension between them contrasted sadly with the euphoria of their wedding day two weeks earlier. Not that the intervening days or nights had staunched the romanticism of either bride or groom. Diverted it maybe but no more for, however ill-matched in other ways, the ffordes were both postgraduates in fantasy. Caroline for instance, though contemptuous of such fripperies as choir and bells had, nevertheless, no intention of arriving as any hum-drum next-on-the-list bride at the Registry Office. If it was sad that her parents were out of town when the young couple applied for a Special Licence this was offset by her mother having neglected to pack various credit cards before leaving for a holiday in Scotland. Caroline herself refused to believe that the treatment of an only daughter would be grudging so it was little more than anticipation of the event to sign her mother's name when picking up a Harrod's mink coat.

This may have impressed the Registrar. It certainly convinced Roy that he was about to splice himself to a family able to maintain him in that station in life to which he'd encouraged his fantasies to call him.

Roy's own upbringing had not been dull. Before his twelfth birthday his parents had agreed that he was uncontrollable. Any tears they stifled as he was driven away to a school for Wayward Youths were strictly for the neighbours. At Hornblower House young Roy was easy on the scruples and nimble with his tongue.

When he was fifteen he was picked out for a country holiday by a retired Admiral. The old salt had a blue and hungry stare and hairy restless fingers. After sugary cocoa had been served in his den, his glasses misted with good-fellowship and his gestures became increasingly chummy. While Roy found such evenings interesting and the pocket-money useful, he considered the Admiral's factotum – former Able Bodied Seaman Boscobel – much more dashing. Boscobel, strong, silent and loyal tended to ignore him. This summer pattern continued for a couple of years until the Admiral thoughtlessly died, withering the hopes Roy was beginning to formulate by leaving his entire estate (unsuitably, Roy heard at the funeral) to former A.B. Boscobel.

All too soon after, young Roy returned despondently to his parents in a drab Victorian suburb. He took an undemanding job in the city. Since it paid scarcely a pittance each Friday he began to offer himself at weekends as a charming guide to mature American visitors. When the dollar depreciated against Middle Eastern currencies he studied classical Arabic by cassette. Those sheiks who had become his clients were somewhat nonplussed to find themselves chatting to a young Englishman who sounded like a walking version of the Koran but Roy's accommodating charm repaid both their patience and the cost of hiring a room overlooking the Thames for a short time in the afternoons.

Alas, when one invests in youthful bloom alone, one should be aware of the law of diminishing returns. Came the daunting cocktail hour when a princeling, concealing a teenage welter-weight in his shower, escorted Roy back to the lift with the challenging question, 'What are you going to do with the rest of your life, now that you're losing your looks?' Some twenty-fifth birthday gift.

Whatever the answer to the question, Roy was certain it was not in a further forty years grind among the invoices. He considered the advantages of a speedy and profitable marriage. One Harley Street specialist with whom he'd shared a halcyon weekend would, he felt sure, applaud such an intention as a milestone in his sexual career. Mr and Mrs Ford in their simple terraced cottage were relieved when their son began to talk of settling. Though he was evasive when pressed for a snap of his intended they dismissed it as shyness and Mr Ford made over all the interest on his Post Office savings so that the lad could augment his wardrobe and redeem his watch.

Our hero then cultivated the nicer type of tea-shop that lingers in Mayfair and Belgravia. Though the annual carnival of debutantes is now no more than an historical footnote, each year still burgeons with our English roses. Roy did not have to linger long before he noted the winsome Caroline at a nearby table. And Caroline noticed him. Happening to find themselves in the same spot the following day, they chatted and made a date. Roy hocked his watch again and – soon after – a few of his mother's trinkets. Pensioners such as his parents, he supposed very reasonably, rarely dressed for supper.

When Caroline paraded her mink a week before the wedding, Roy realised he must match the stake.

'Which would you prefer darling, a mini-honeymoon in Brussels straight after the Hilton reception or shall we wait and do the thing properly in the Bahamas in the Spring?'

'Can't we give Brussels a miss, Roy? It really is the Hounslow of Europe. I'll be happy with a weekend at the Hilton, and Nassau around Easter.'

They agreed on this modest compromise though it was not exactly the case Roy presented to his father that night. Understanding that air fares do have to be paid in advance, Mr Ford produced his cheque book. Mrs Ford paused from her mending to repeat that she did so hope she'd soon be meeting her future daughter-in-law. Next morning Roy reserved the Bridal Suite overlooking Hyde Park. So little cash was left in these inflationary times, that it barely covered the champagne breakfasts to be served during their stay.

Insulated from London's traffic they enjoyed a weekend of modern delight. Roy realised early that the dream is half the adventure and Caroline was quick to accept that her husband's hesitancy in bed illustrated exactly the nervousness of the male virgin so praised in the work of Barbara Cartland. She was, of course, half-right. Too soon it was time to set about leasing a serviced flat within strolling distance of the West End. Having found a suitable mews, there was the dreary necessity of offering a quarter's rent in advance. Caroline's parents, far from seeming irate at their daughter's speedy marriage, had still not returned from Scotland.

'No problem,' laughed Roy, 'I'll have another word with my father.' Grabing a brochure from the Belgian State Tourist Bureau en route, Roy dashed home for the evening. Over supper he was colourfully expansive about the honeymoon in Brussels and seemingly informed about the Common Market. After helping with the washing-up he explained to his parents that the substantial cheque he needed was a mere loan until his rich in-laws returned from their loch-side estates. Mrs Ford hoped she'd soon be drinking a cup of tea in the newly-weds flat and Mr Ford saw his bank manager the following morning to arrange for an advance on his railwayman's pension.

'No problem darling. Just as I told you,' Roy smiled, finishing a well-jugged hare, 'they'd hardly expect me to live off my wife.'

Caroline squeezed her husband's thigh intimately in a way that reminded him for a second of the deceased Admiral. 'I'm so delighted you're not a drone Roy, sheltering behind all this sex-equality twaddle. By the way, I rang Daddy last night and let him have our new number. There was one other thing. I did want to confirm with him the details of great-aunt Lavinia's Will. It was her one recurring wish that she should furnish my first home. Roy, my dearest, tomorrow we go to Harrods.'

They did and since drizzling rain had been forecast they took a taxi. Caroline explained that it would be a trifling expediency, nothing more, to charge all goods to her mother's account since great-aunt Lavinia's inheritance could be made over as quick as a signature.

'Tell me more of your great-aunt,' Roy smiled as they lunched in the restaurant.

'Enormously rich my darling. Quite stuffy with it.'

'But will it have to be shared round the family,' Roy spoke artlessly to a forkful of asparagus, 'now that the old bird's croaked?'

'But my dearest dear, I told you. Or I meant to. Every brass penny showers down on little me.'

'How long ago did she snuff it?'

'Four months? I forget exactly . . . it was all too distressing. I tried to save her – naturally – but the current was too strong.'

They considered the strength of tides in the Bahamas over coffee and the possibility of sharks. Having signed the bill, Caroline guided her husband towards the water-beds. Later they split, Caroline making for Aspreys to discuss silver goblets and Roy for their flat where he dozed after the draining experience of the morning's shopping. The phone rang and his mother-in-law announced herself.

'Well, hello Mother,' he cut in in his chattiest manner, 'welcome back frae bonnie Scotland. I feel I should call you Mother though we've not yet met.'

'Get young Carrie to this phone in two ticks or there's a thing or two I might call you.'

'My wife is out shopping. Is there something wrong?'

'Two bloody thousand pounds wrong my laddie. Tell her to phone me back before she gets that mink off her shoulders.'

'How's Caroline's father?' Roy's tone was solicitous. An interest in family health he'd always found to be a trustworthy lightning conductor.

'I don't know and I care less. I've not clapped eyes on the creature in ten years I'm happy to say.'

With this disconcerting reply the receiver was banged down.

'Caroline, my little love,' Roy said as he poured her rum and coke, 'that photo of your parents implies that they are living together.'

'And that is how I like to think of them dearest. I just can't think why Mummy is in such a state. Perhaps I should pop over and see her.'

'Just as you think, dearest. I do hope all is well with the Will. I shall have to let my father have that money back.'

'Surely he'd not grudge it to us, my sweet?'

'Well of course not. It's no more than a flea-bite but it might come in handy when they go on holiday next week.'

'They're going away? I was so hoping to meet them soon. They sound such a dear old Derby and Joan. Roy when am I going to see your cricket cups and things?'

'Just as soon as Ma and Pa are back. Talking of which, shouldn't you nip over to your Mother's?'

Caroline was more subdued than Roy had ever known her to be when she returned. She even wondered if perhaps they should not have delayed the wedding.

'What about the cheque?' Roy demanded.

'Filthy money. That's all you ever think about,' Caroline screamed with unsuspected vigour. 'I just hope you've not been camouflaging a nasty middle-class streak. We'll have the piddling money in plenty of time for the Bahamas.'

'I was rather thinking about next week's bus fares.'

For the first time, Roy slept on the chesterfield.

When he was leaving for work the following morning Caroline called pleasantly, 'Pick up some more rum and gin on your way home darling.'

Roy called at his bank to inspect the ledger sheet. It was raw and angry.

At work he pleaded an upset stomach. It was worth weathering the grins and innuendoes to be given the afternoon off. By two o'clock he was drinking with his old friend the Harley Street consultant. By four, conversation was minimal and by eight – after a light supper – he was twenty pounds better off and in a cab on his way home. Caroline was already in bed and very sulky.

'I rang your office,' she observed, blowing smoke rings at the ceiling, 'you've not been there since lunch. How is the upset stomach? I hope your whoring in some suburban bedroom has

68

cheered it up.'

'Don't be suspicious darling. I've been seeing my parents off to Turkey.'

'I'm so unhappy,' Caroline snivelled, 'I've been left alone all day and bloody Aspreys have sent a bill for those goblets already.'

'So what? Everythings's on lamented aunt Lavinia, isn't it?'

'And I expect you've forgotten the gin. I need another drink.'

'Later my sweetest. You know, I think we should go and inspect the details of that Will.'

'My great-aunt lived in Greensleeves Minor. That's a hell of a way Roy and I'm too unhappy to discuss it further,' Caroline snapped and flicked off the reading light.

Roy switched it on.

'Not that far, I'm sure,' he smiled, fingering twenty fresh pound notes and shifting his arse to a softer part of the duvet. 'I'll take Friday off and we can toddle down. Where exactly is the village?'

'Look the dump up for yourself. Anyway, I'm doing something important on Friday.'

'Indeed you are darling. We shall both be together all day.'

But they did not sleep together that night.

Caroline had a migraine just after dawn the following Friday so they did not catch the nine fifteen. She appeared to have mislaid her lipstick so Roy dashed out to buy a replacement though it did mean losing the ten fifteen.

An hour later, however, they were travelling first class next to the dining car and the bar on the inter-city train west to Exeter. There they changed to a branch line that wound through Crediton to Greensleeves Minor. Though it may have been an Eden on the slopes of Dartmoor at midsummer, the straggling village was none too welcoming in lashing rain.

Mr Smedley the solicitor was quite amazed that they should have made so challenging a journey on so miserable a day.

'There's really so very little I can tell you Miss . . . forgive me, Mrs fforde. The balance of what monies are due to you personally will be forwarded in rather less than two months. You can't be unaware that I've made certain advances already to your mother against your own written undertaking to repay. As for what remains, I very much fear the pair of you must have spent almost half of it trekking down here to see us on this unpleasant afternoon.'

Caroline, apparently unconcerned, inspected her nail-varnish critically. Roy was stupified and Mr Smedley, sensing something amiss, spoke directly to him. 'Tell me, Mr fforde, would your first name by any chance be Roy?'

'If it adds a couple of noughts to the account we're due: yes, it is. Why?'

'I'm something of a new boy here Mr fforde. My wife and I find Dartmoor more relaxing than the strains of Winchester. It occured to me a second ago that it must be all of six years now since I wound up Admiral Pomeroy's estate. You do so put me in mind of a lad I glimpsed once or twice at his place. I could swear it was Roy Ford. But then you spell your name with two ffs and an e, so it could hardly have been you, could it?'

'Pity,' Roy smiled and very casually inspected his watch. 'The old boy might have left me a pound or two.'

'I hardly think so. Everything went to his faithful friend Harry Boscobel. I still have a Christmas card from him every year. Harry sold the estate of course. Wanted the London life . . . well takes all sorts. Nice to think the money didn't turn his head. He lives quite modestly down Chiswich way he tells me.'

'Nice for him but it doesn't help us, Mr Smedley,' Caroline laughed. Turning to Roy she added, 'I think we should be making for the station darling.'

'How right you are, dearest. We shall never make Cornwall at this rate,' Roy joked. To Mr Smedley he said, 'I've only just realised. While we've been chatting here, the banks will have closed for the weekend. Any chance you could be kind enough to cash me a cheque for fifty pounds?'

'I'm sure that can be arranged,' Smedley purred, calculating he held twice that amount as Caroline's residual inheritance.

'I'm beginning to have some nasty doubts about you,' shouted Caroline as they floundered through slashing rain towards Greensleeves Halt. 'You told me you were at school at Wellington.'

'Just head for the station and keep puzzling, little Caro,' Roy shouted back as he bounded a flooded gutter, 'Might have been Wellington Street School for Wayward Youths. More to the point let's discuss your evaporating wealth.'

'Are we really going to Cornwall then?'

'That fifty pounds I cashed, dearest wife, is to keep me in fares and you in eggs and chips until the far side of never.'

There, for some hours, all conversation ended. Until they were well on the way to Paddington to be exact. Even then speech was functional – limited to the choice between cheese and tomato and ham and tomato sandwiches for supper. When the train stopped Roy grabbed two copies of the evening paper as the bookstall shutters were being pulled down.

'There,' he snapped, aiming one at Caroline, 'I'm going to the loo. Start searching for a bedsitter. Something we can afford between the gasworks and the pickle factory.'

He left his wife not too far from the taxi rank, cantered down to a cubicle, closed the seat cover to make himself relatively comfortable and began work on the crossword. After some twenty minutes he flushed the loo, buttoned his coat and nipped back to the concourse once more. He wasn't dismayed to find that Caroline had disappeared. In the station buffet he bought himself a lager and, when he'd sipped it down, strolled to the phone booth. He rang the flat but there was no answer. Roy rang his mother-in-law. 'Not here' was the terse comment and he guessed his voice had been recognised. That, he thought, most probably means she is.

He thumbed the A to D directory, found H. Boscobel and dialled a Chiswick address. 'Harry Boscobel here,' he heard. It was sufficient. He whistled all the way to the taxi-rank.

'Ninety three, The Riverside, Chiswick,' he said.

Twenty minutes later at the boat-house by the corner, he paid off the cab and, huddling under the willows, made his way to the gate of ninety three. There was a light in the porch outlining the man who stood at the door. Roy recognised his build immediately.

From the gateway he also recognised the voice of the bedraggled young woman who was calling through the rain,

'I really do apologise for knocking you up but my sports car broke down near the fly-over. A dear old Derby and Joan couple gave me a lift to your corner. Do you think I might possibly come in and telephone my mother, Lady Lavinia fforde?'

PEPPERMINT FUDGE

I was certain I would never be happy in the house and regretted that Miss Marchant had left it to my father. She despised me as a weakling, that I knew. Equally, though not as a consequence, I disliked her. I hated the way in which she'd muzzled in on our family: adopting us at first and then, during the five years that we knew her, suggesting with ever-increasing outspokeness how we should live our lives. That's what happens when one of your parents starts chatting to eccentric old ladies at Jumble Sales. Throughout the years I was at Primary School I was dragged, once a month, to Sunday afternoon tea at Miss Marchant's. The only high spot that made those duty visits bearable was the delicious peppermint fudge she made and stored in an orange tin box.

Six months after her funeral, my father received the keys of the house. Being eleven and a half by then, I didn't care to admit that I was terrified of the Victorian villa in which an old woman had happened to die. I wouldn't even let my mother suspect that I would have gone to the dentist three times rather than pass a blustery December afternoon alone in the place, measuring all the windows for the new curtains she was planning. My father had already been over there half a dozen times at weekends repainting the inside from attics to cellars but – being a methodical man – he'd not yet tackled Miss Marchant's bedroom. As I clambered up and down his step-ladder jotting measurements in a race against the failing light, I could still detect – lingering in the alcoves of her room – the harsh savour of her no-nonsense soap.

Although I'd seen her grave and knew that six feet of London

73

clay rested on her, I had to fight the feeling that those eyes of hers, glittering like guardsmens' buttons, weren't following me to the window. The slow drip of a distant tap reminded me of Miss Marchant champing her hideous false teeth throughout those Sunday afternoons. I'd always felt, sitting opposite her, as a puppy must do when being surveyed by a mastiff. Well, she might have despised me then because I intended to be an architect, rather than a soldier like all her own relatives, but I knew enough of military manoeuvres that December afternoon not to cut off my retreat. I'd left her bedroom door wide open – and the street door downstairs too – on the off chance that I might panic and run.

I'll admit I'd left her room until last so, with the last measurement noted, it was by the light of the passing traffic that I backed from the windows across the linoleum towards the landing. Just as I reached the doorway, my heel scuffed a solid object in the corner. It rattled and I froze until I could no longer hear the echo. Keeping my eyes fixed on the windows and the commuters beyond reading their evening papers on the buses, I gradually felt down and down until I touched something metallic. Would you believe I almost sobbed with relief? It was only the orange tin box that was once crammed with home-made fudge.

Imagine the reassurance of that moment. I had deluded myself that there was any menace in the empty house. More than that, Miss Marchant just couldn't have been the hostile figure I'd supposed her to be – ever-ready for opportunities to make me feel nervous or inadequate. Quite simply, she'd been a lonely old woman, glad of a family in which she could take some interest and thoughtful enough to leave me something special before she died – some chunks of her delicious peppermint fudge which would, with luck, not have become too stale.

The street door banged as the wind got up again but I didn't care. In the quietness of the bedroom I prised up the lid of the tin to gather up some lumps that I could munch on my way home. My fingers groped further, exploring the darkest corner and there they closed, expectantly, on the cold porcelain of Miss Marchant's spare false teeth.

SOME LIKE COFFEE AND SOME LIKE TEA

It was the clinking of milk bottles that disturbed Hal's dream. Rarely conscious of domestic developments until Pat brought in a tray of tea, he sensed a subtle difference about the morning. Pat, respectful of Hal's insecurities, habitually kept their bedroom door shut. Unaccountably it was open as was the stripped pine door that divided the living room from the minute hall. From the arctic draught that flurried the bedroom curtains it was certain that the street door was open too.

Hal didn't resent the disturbance. With his first full surge of consciousness he realised it was Celebration Friday. A first cigarette in bed before being caught up in the swirl of events would, he reasoned, be a pardonable luxury. He could even enjoy the breakfast chat-show. His own remarkable triumph was sure to be mentioned: even analysed by some garrulous pollster. Reaching for Pat's pillow to prop himself up he found it oddly cold to the touch. The previous evening replayed before him instantly. The very last stipulation he'd made to Pat before nipping off in his own car to the Town Hall had been, 'Listen, love, I know we've never discussed it and we should have done but – if I win – low profile, eh? Just while things are sorted a bit. Come to that, lie low if I lose.'

The transistor still silent in his fist, Hal wriggled anxiously across the divan until he could squint through the gloom and the open doorways to the street entrance. His heart vaulted with such force that he feared he might well be the first member to expire in the moment of victory. Obviously Pat had flouted all instructions. There was no mistaking those ash-blond curls even in the grisliest of dawns. Yet how – unless set on their mutual destruction – could Pat have gone to collect the milk and papers, exposing himself to neighbours and constituents alike, in a quilted morning coat that wouldn't have meritted fifth prize in a holiday camp contest?

'What the hell are you at?' he yelled with a throatiness acquired through three weeks at the hustings. 'Five bloody years I nurse this seat with charm and discretion. Must you blow the bloody lot in two minutes giving the world a drag show?' The distant figure straightened and turned. Arms weighed with milk and papers, mouth and pockets stuffed with cables and letters, it tripped back through the gloom of the untidy living room. Even when pissed enough to parody the Prime Minister, Pat never darted about as purposefully. The realisation comforted Hal not at all.

'Hey . . . you. Who the hell are you?'

No reply from the kitchen.

'Listen,' screeched Hal bounding naked over the bedroom floor, 'are you some agent provacateur hired to splatter my private life across the weekend papers?' Fearing if this were so there might be an accomplice, camera at the ready, Hal wrenched both hook and dressing gown from behind the bedroom door.

'Cool it, Hal. Easy now. Coffee's almost ready.'

The vocal similarity was unnerving with just that sexy mezzo quality Pat affected when imitating newscasters.

'Out,' Hal yelled as he scrabbled under cushions and coffee-tables for tape recorders or bugs, 'out this instant.' He paused with a table lamp in one hand. 'No. dress yourself properly first. You can borrow that unassuming charcoal I wear for Masonic lunches. And don't forget your bloody chauffeur's cap . . . oh, shit,' he concluded, opening the curtains on a landscape softened by drizzle, 'what's the point? You're not Pat anyway.'

He swung angrily to the kitchen doorway and raised both arms, barring any escape. 'So, who the hell are you and – more to the point – how did you get in?'

'Easy Hal. Now, milk with coffee first thing in the morning and cream after supper: I have got it right, haven't I? Attention to detail is the hallmark of the professional: our first lesson,' smiled the stranger turning to face Hal in a robe loose enough to display most of two firm breasts. He contrived not to look. Instead he shouted at the ironing board.

'That's not your hair. It takes more than a wig to deceive me. I don't know who you are or what you're at but Pat you most certainly are not . . .'

'But I am, Hal, I am. That is, I'm Patricia . . . not Patrick I admit. I'm from Establishment Cover Services – E.C.S. – at your beck and call from now on to protect your image. Does the coffee look right? Do have some – you may need it to fortify yourself a little. Where was I? O, yes, my name. It was felt that in the heat of the next few days you might forgetfully refer to Pat . . . so, here I am. My, you do look peaky. I'd say have a drop more sugar but my list says you're a weight watcher.'

Hal slumped against the fridge, 'Am I never to be allowed to be myself again? 'he moaned, barely conscious that a mug was being edged towards his lips. Pushing it away so aggressively that coffee slopped on his toes he yelped, 'So just how did you force your way in?'

'Let's not be naïve, Hal. We at E.C.S. do work in close liason with all public bodies, not least your own political party. Naturally we keep abreast,' Patricia folded her dressing gown a little tighter, 'abreast of new techniques. Was that your doorbell? Thought so. It'll be the photographic agencies waiting to catch me unawares in deshabille. That had to be fixed last night the minute the result was declared. Won't be a mo.'

'You're not going to my door like that? What do you suppose my gay supporters will make of it in the evening papers?'

'What a sweet old fashioned thought, Hal. They voted yester-day, didn't they, not today? A little pinch of pragmatism never comes amiss in public service: lesson thirteen at E.C.S. Don't let your coffee get cold.'

Hal hoisted himself onto the kitchen table in despair. Why, he reproached himself, had he never made the moment to discuss with Pat – his Pat for four whole years – a situation for which he was pathetically unprepared? Thrust into the public gaze by an unexpected result in an unforeseen by-election nothing had been thought through. Except, very obviously, by some shadowy figure at Party Headquarters who, having done some positive vetting work had whisked the matter out of Hal's hands to keep the party's image sweet as roses and drop Hal Brimacombe's private life in the shit.

Withered in the bud those assurances to gay activists that, if they'd support him, he would soon enough speak out for them. So much for the young herald of a new dawn in which bedroom preferences would count no more or less than pigmentation or a predeliction for lemon tea. The pass had been sold before he'd even reached Westminster and kissed hands or whatever antique ritual he had to perform.

'Hal darling,' Patricia's voice trilled from the street door, 'the boys want a shot of us together.'

Hal was aware, as he trudged to join her, that he was picking at himself as though attempting to remove a mask that was already adherring.

'Can't you forget that shaving rash a moment? They won't mind your beard any more than I do,' Patricia simpered, dropping both arms about his neck and dangling a cable from one hand. The youth who had delivered it lingered to stare at Hal with more interest than he'd shown at a recent disco.

'A smile please Mr Brimacombe,' grunted a photographer, 'think of the happy day. When's it to be or are you going to be our first trendy open member?'

'Our what?' Hal gawped into the lights.

'The first back-bencher to live in open sin.'

'You'll have to wait and see, just as Asquith advised, 'Hal spoke with seeming joviality as he sank hidden nails into Patricia's ribs. Her smile hardened almost imperceptibly for she was a trooper and her expenses were tax free. It shouldn't be supposed that Hal was sadistic. He withdrew his grip apologetically for in reappraising the situation he judged Patricia a fellow victim – possibly an ally – against the shadowy Dodos who were trying to crank the rusting machine of pretence at whatever cost.

'Sorry love,' he breathed in her ear. Turning to the photographer he enjoyed the decisiveness of public office for the first time, 'Right chaps, that's it. Breakfast and a shave now then the next train to London.'

As he closed the door both of them could smell toast singeing in the kitchen.

'Listen Patricia,' Hal observed flapping fumes towards the open window, 'how long are you under contract to me for? We can't seriously prolong this farce for ever.'

Patricia finished scraping the toast in a manner searingly reminiscent of Patrick. 'The good of the Party is paramount, that's my brief. We don't want any more minor calamities like Lord Hamlett, do we? Speaking of whom, how do you like your eggs done?'

'I'd rather you didn't mention me in the same breath as that psychotic careerist. Perhaps you'd better not speak at all until I've sorted out what's to be done. Be useful and pop on some soothing music. Make it English . . . Britten maybe or Tippett . . .'

'Hal, don't you think maybe . . .?'

'O very well. Make it Elgar stamping over the wolds in a muffler if you must.' The cello was no sooner soaring with Edwardian certainty and Hal's bathwater swirling than the doorbell sounded a second time. Patricia, tripping away to answer it, was curiously silent. Hal dimmed the hot-water tap and Sir Edward and made after her. 'Patricia, of all people,' a well-loved voice was saying, 'four years no-see then here you are in my own home . . . and so informally dressed.'

Hal pushed past both figures to close the front door with a crash.

'And just what brings you here anyway? Is my word less than nothing? Who was to maintain a low profile? Who was booked into the Y.M.C.A. for three nights?' Patrick – for it was none other – began his explanation meekly enough. Being in some matters sluggish he was not at his nimblest in early morning rows.

'Hal I do promise you no one saw me. I crept up the fire escape and threw a dustbin lid over the balcony to distract some Post Office youth who was loitering.'

He paused and, lighting a cigarette, glanced first at Patricia who was once more tightening her dressing gown and then at Hal who stood in full-frontal nudity. He became bolder.

'Need I have bothered I ask myself? What little bit of hanky-panky have I disturbed dearest Hal?'

'Now just you listen one moment . . .'

'Don't try any of your "I know thee not, old man," number on me Hal Brimacombe. I see it all. If I hadn't been educated simply in a comprehensive school I would have guessed you with your boarding school deviousness would end up marrying your lover's sister. In this instance cousin before you pick me up on accuracy . . .'

'Your *cousin* . . .?'

'He's right Hal, we are related,' Patricia smiled leading Patrick who had begun to sniff noisily into the living room. 'Now Patrick just understand that I let myself in with a key less than an hour ago. Your key possibly. It was you who gave a police cadet a lift a couple of weeks a go, wasn't it?'

'Not in the campaign car?' Hal groaned.

'Well I got bored sitting at the back of your meetings to give you heckling practice. Anyway, he had bad breath.'

'We'll discuss that in depth some time. Meanwhile, listen. Patricia here has been sent by some wretched busybodies to make me as publicly acceptable as toothpaste. Whoever they are make the K.G.B. and C.I.A. look as efficient as the Mother's Union. Patrick do stop snivelling. Patricia, how long have you been working for Establishment Coverups?'

'Establishment Cover Services please. Not that long . . .'

'I thought,' Patrick said accusingly between blowing his nose loudly, 'you were an out of work actress doing platform announcements for British Rail.'

'Still am. This is a sort of leave of absence for work of national importance. E.C.S. gives one the chance to meet such colourful figures: Generals with a penchant for diving suits and Duchesses who insist they're poodles. Our job is to match the client's requirements to our resources and take ten per cent from the punter.'

'The whole monstrous artifice must be exposed,' Hal fumed.

'O come now, why disturb the status quo . . . delicacy prevents me naming . . .'

'Is there no honesty left in England? Listen Patricia, count me out, eh? I will not join. I'm gay G-A-Y and that's the way I'll stay. Pat what the hell are you doing in my bath?'

'I could be slitting my throat for all you care. If you come on in I'll do your back. Tricia won't mind.'

Hal turned to Patricia for a final appeal.

'Listen love. Couldn't you, not for my sake or for Christ's sake but for honesty's sake grab your glad-rags and go? I intend to blow this little plot apart when I hit London so an hour or two is neither here nor there.'

'We're all free agents Hal . . .'

'Are we? You really are a giggle a minute Patricia. The least you can do is give me a cigarette.'

Patricia willingly rummaged in the pocket of her dressing gown under a crumpled cable. It was unfortunate that a rather cheap ostentatious engagement ring rolled onto the carpet with her cigarette lighter. Patricia looked up first.

'I can explain Hal.'

'And rather quickly I think.'

'Well you see,' Patricia, rather glad that her acting course had included a generous amount of training in improvisation, 'I wanted to save the public embarrassment . . .'

'There's an unsuspected streak of humanity in you love . . .'

'. . . so I thought I'd break it gently that Sylvan Television are on their way to do an interview and, if we're not engaged by the time they arrive, Aurora Grillinger will produce a ring from their property department and we'll have to do it live on the air.'

Undecided whether to scream or laugh, Hal stood waving both his arms in a helpless circular movement.

'I don't think,' he said finally, 'I shall go straight to Westminster. I shall go quite coolly, very soberly to Party Head-quarters and I shall strangle whoever has devised this laundering of my personality.'

There was a knock at the door. The bell sounded twice. Patricia looked through the window and along the balcony then shook her head at Hal. He grinned, folded his arms.

'Go and do some more improvising, 'he suggested. 'Tell them I'll be interviewed on the thirty first of never, meanwhile they can piss off.'

It was only when the television team, protesting loudly, had withdrawn that Hal and Patricia were aware of Patrick's dripping figure, sherry bottle in hand, at the bathroom doorway.

'So,' he said waspishly, kicking the chaise-longue to underline his words, 'I'm destined to be hidden like a nasty smell in some attic on the wrong side of the river, am I? A bit of sly nonsense when there's no big debate on, is that it?'

'Will you be reasonable . . .'

'No. I see it all, Hal Brimacombe. You've used me and your gay voters as a vaulting horse in your career. Now it's turn the clocks back to the Furtive Fifties, isn't it?'

'Patrick, don't get emotional. Pour us all a stiff one. As for you, Patricia, I'm not entirely convinced the engagement bit wouldn't be a step up in your career.'

'Why should I want you? It isn't in my contract. I should hope I could manage something better than a back-bencher shared with my own cousin.'

Patrick, about to accuse her of anything for publicity, was prevented from doing so by the phone bell. Patricia picked up the receiver and, after a moment, passed it to Hal.

'Personnel department at Party Headquarters. Dudley Ploy, he said.'

'Never heard of him . . . this is Hal Brimacombe. Who you are I neither know nor care. Just get this and get it good. I'm not engaged. I'm not marrying Patricia Whosit. You and the bloody camera team you sent down can get stuffed separately or together as the mood takes you. I trust I make myself clear?'

The line was not good but the sigh from the London end was gently audible. From the voice that began to chide Hal could conjure a face not particularly to his liking. One he had since childhood associated, erroneously, with the core of another political party. A face bred from beautiful women and assured if not intelligent men. A face that guided England whichever way the voters wandered. Dudley Ploy Hal surmised was, like Walt Whitman, large enough to accommodate contradictions and he, Hal Brimacombe, was less than a tiny anomaly to be attended to before lunch at the Club.

'And if you would just listen a moment,' the unflurried voice continued, 'I'm sure you wish to enjoy a full term at Westminster so if I were you I'd just take the eleven thirty and you'll be here by three. With Patricia. Take my point?'

'I'll bloody say I do, Dud. If I may call you Dud. Just before I tell you to sod off, remember I'm accountable to the voters of Greensleeves Major, not to you, Dud. If I want to waltz through Whitehall with Patricia on one arm and Patrick on the other I'll do so. Take my point?'

'That reminds me Hal. Your opponent's agent most kindly returned a pair of chauffeur's gloves. It is somewhat irregular to lend campaign cars to other parties on Declaration Night. You are of course entitled to take a different view of lending out your friend . . .'

Hal glowered at Patrick, covered the mouthpiece and hissed, 'I'll have a word or two with you you virtuous trollop . . .'

Regaining his composure Hal snapped back at Dudley that his private life was entirely his own business.

'Not exactly how the Press may see it Hal. You're the brightest young hope for many a Parliament you know. Wouldn't wish to have your image tarnished with gossip about your membership of Beckfords Club, or that indiscrete moment in the Public Bar of the Lord Hervey? I take it you'll list the study of derelict windmills on the Common at midnight among your interests in Who's Who?' Hal had had enough.

'Listen, you establishment hit man,' he yelled, 'go and drip your slimy muck wherever you want. Joe and Joan Public are a bloody sight more open minded than you and your little prep school pals. The hell with your naughtiness and guilt. All that's behind me like this morning's shit. Take a tip Dud and start listening to what smelly, laughing humanity thinks, not what Sunday editors crawling for knighthoods want them to think.'

Hal slammed the phone onto its cradle, rubbed his hands and, grinning, picked up his drink. Patricia smiled openly at him for the first time and Patrick sheepishly refilled their glasses.

'Sorry Hal. I mean about last night. I did want you. Pity he was your opponent's researcher. Apart from nice nostrils he wasn't much of a turn on.'

'Forget everything,' Hal said and drained his glass decisively. 'It's all over: or maybe just beginning. We go to London. All three. I'll have two tickets for the Public Gallery this afternoon. One for Patrick my researcher; the other for his cousin who has worked so hard behind the scenes. Let's get dressed and head for the shit or bust trail.'

'By the way,' Patricia said as they settled in a quiet compartment, 'I was told to give you these for emergencies.'

Hal examined the gold rimmed spectacles which very obviously were devised for the chronically short-sighted.

'Why the hell? I see well enough.'

'They know that. They're a sort of insurance policy in case you cuddle Patrick by mistake instead of me. We explain you're myopic. Worked for one colonial Prime Minister for years, I'm told.'

And so the newly elected member for Greensleeves Major arrived at Westminster. Two Privy Counsellors added gravitas as the party of three moved from the Bar of the House of Commons to decorous murmurs of 'Hear, hear,' not only from Hal's own party but from all who felt that so comely and upstanding a young man might put them in touch with all the fresh ideas that were reputed to be blowing in the breezes. Hal signed the book and stepped forward to shake hands with Mr Speaker – a man whose sprightly and perceptive humour was not obvious, leading the lightminded to dismiss him as a clothes peg on loan from a theatrical costumiers.

'I look forward to knowing you better, Mr Brimacombe,' he said genially. Maybe to put the new member at ease he added, 'Is that

Pat in the gallery watching?' The man, Hal realised, was thorough in his homework. How thorough? Certainly Hal was thrown sufficiently to burble, 'Yes he is. That is, she is. Or rather they are.'

'All rather confusing isn't it, at first?' Mr Speaker sympathised with a momentary twinkle before his dismissive bow. In long years of office he'd welcomed a saint or two and rather more sinners.

Hal Brimacombe gulped, turned to take a not very prominent seat and smiled up once towards the Public Gallery. Mr Speaker, too, was reseating himself. 'An interesting moment,' he confided to the mace below him. The mace didn't even tremble.

A LYRIC QUALITY

My taste may be dismissed as coarse – vulgar even – but I have never cared for English lyric tenors. Osbert Hargreaves' voice reinforced my opinion. There was, for me, less discomfort in lying sleepless because of a wailing, unsatisfied tomcat than in being exposed to his thin, sexless performance. To be plain, I was never convinced he'd one semi-quaver of music in him. Technique of course: forty adult years of that behind him before he was killed. There was little else, believe me. Since I've admitted to coarseness and vulgarity I may well add (having heard him in oratorios and on the radio) that I could never be sure he had any balls.

Perhaps it was the fluting, antiseptic quality in his singing – odd and disturbing to me – that so turned-on middle-aged and elderly ladies. They certainly seethed by the coachload at ticket offices wherever he was giving a recital. Hargreaves was never one for operatic appearances. Which Carmen worth her castanets could have had a stage affair that suspended one second's disbelief with him? As for Callas, she would have minced and scoffed him for cocktail snacks during the overture.

Hargreaves was most at home in murky churches and cathedrals. His singing matched the fanvaulting above him: clear, precise and chillingly faultless. Maybe not always faultless. We're coming to that. Little was known of Hargreaves off the platform – the man inside the dinner jacket as it were – other than that his music, his town garden and his enthusiasm as a teacher of boy sopranos were all his life. Who can say or tell whether he was hypersensitive to criticism of his tubs of chrysanthemums? He most certainly was when confronted with adverse press notices about his recitals. One hostile phrase, just one, was sufficient for him to cancel all bookings for three months, tend his garden, work extra hours with pupils who converged from twenty miles around London and – during this self-imposed retreat he would – as he revealed in a rare television interview – diet wholly on his special broth.

This extended tantrum which he had dignified as a ritual began sometime after his fiftieth birthday for it was then that one jumped-up young critic had dared imply that Osbert Hargreaves might have passed his peak. Three months later that young man was forced to swallow his suggestion. Hargreaves bounced back as he did at fifty five, sixty and sixty five. Scrubbed and confident, he'd reappear to trill his way through a cycle of the better known sea-shanties or a posy of bowdlerised folk-songs. When this first happened, Fleet Street's musicologists swore all the way to the corner bar. 'The old bugger's done it. What's he on? Drugs? Hypnosis? Monkey-glands?'. They were wrong, every frayed and battered one of them including the young freelance who covered such events from *Forum*. He told a saucy joke about Dame Nellie Melba, the Covent Garden stage-hands and voice lubrication. Not that anyone believed it since everyone knows them all to be sex-mad at *Forum*. Following Hargreaves second rejuvenation, that same young freelance was not at the corner bar to stand his round. Bright lad, he was at the artists' entrance asking the singer to what he attributed his startlingly firm attack that evening. 'Practice and then more practice dear boy. And, of course, two daily cups of my home brewed broth.'

Now although it happens seldom it cannot be ruled out that the scribblers who devise our television commercials can also read. An impoverished young poet who'd sunk from Fabers to writing limericks for Underground posters finally divorced his muse and took a job with an advertising agency. Among other projects this company was responsible for launching the campaign for a new brand of soup on undernourished viewers. Idling in his attic office one morning, the former revolutionary poet read in his upmarket paper of Hargreaves' latest come back. Why not, he mused, involve this very English figure in the promotion of the new soup-powder?

Hargreaves was, initially, coy. How could he reconcile the brash vulgarity of a tele-ad with the fastidiousness of his refined and slightly donnish public? Again – he hedged – he didn't actually need the money. (He spoke before he'd been told the size of the cheque and the revenue from repeat fees). As for recognition of his standing in the community wasn't he – he comforted himself – due at the Palace within weeks to be made a Companion of something or other?

Finally he accepted but there were provisos. Not financial. Far more crucial was the question of the location and the text. Filming, he insisted, would have to be done in his autumn garden where the gold chrysanthemums 'boomed and rang like gongs' as one admirer had once put it. Hargreaves himself would suspend a sachet of instant chicken broth elegantly from his left hand and a cup of his own secret formula concoction would be poised in his right. The angle, roughly, would be that the punters, if they invested in the new brand might – so help us – sing as blithely as Osbert. Not quite, however, for the star was fuelled from his own home-brew. Nevertheless, should he be pressed for time, he too would settle for the amazing new soup-powder.

There were the predictable delays on shooting day. A downpour drove the camera team indoors and they were compelled to idle around calculating overtime. As everyone moved out once more into the hesitant sunshine, some wretched mother phoned from the suburbs in a state because her son hadn't returned from his singing lesson the previous evening. Osbert, on edge as ever before a performance, snapped at her that as the lad had no sense of pitch anyway he'd probably run off with a rock group. And then, with everything ready to roll, the Steinway was out of tune as a result of the downpour. It was long past midday when the first takes were in the can. Disastrous they were, too. Osbert was jittery and, later that day in the cutting room, the best of twelve attempts had to be married and matched. At home in his Regency villa, the star who'd overheard one or two bitchy asides from the technicians about his manner and his life-style, was shouting at his agent.

Yes, Osbert made himself very clear. All engagements were to be cancelled until December brought its annual whistle-stop progress around the carol concerts. So uneven had his television performance been that he was determined to pass the closing weeks of the year tending his chrysanths, consuming his broth that was chilling in a dozen screw-top jars and coaching his pupils. Keen to exorcise the chaos of the day, he petulantly tipped his year's free supply of the wretched powdered soup into the loo with such distaste that, next morning, it was blocked. His uncomplaining home-help swore the place stank like an abattoir and phoned for a plumber.

Despite a spartan diet, Osbert was down to the last quarter-jar of his own rich, jellied stock by Christmas week. Then it was time to re-emerge, a bright-eyed, unwrinkled pensioner, for one of his more memorable performances. Not joyous, you understand, Hargreaves was never that and his favourite encore – The Coventry Carol – hardly called for the exuberance of a Christmas knees-up.

The slow autumn of daily practice and the frugal bowls of broth were vindicated. There were rave notices and Osbert was busy throughout the holiday answering fan mail. To the parents of his former pupil who had never reappeared he sent condolences and to the parents of a curly headed youth from a high-rise block who he had been training to sing treble solos in Handel's Messiah on Twelfth Night he sent encouragement. 'Your son,' he scrawled, 'although already fifteen, has never sung more purely. Would that we might all retain the crystal Blake-like innocence of youth.'

On Twelfth Night, the lad's parents were in the best box at the Albert Hall. Osbert himself joined them at twenty nine minutes past seven having, as he whispered, been delayed by a phone call from The Palace. At twenty minutes to eight Sir Rupert, who was conducting, wandered on to uncertain applause. The treble soloist could not be found. Osbert reassured the bewildered parents that their son, in an understandable bout of artistic nerves, had probably slipped off to see a space epic. Then he nipped out of the box. Two minutes later Sir Rupert was to be seen in whispered conference and, seconds later, he was asking the indulgence of the audience. Osbert Hargreaves, happening to be in the house, had most kindly agreed to sing the soprano line at the last moment if they agreed. Agreed? The audience, conscious that it was party to the making of musical history, was won before Sir Rupert had flourished his baton.

Not so all the critics. Notices the following morning were very mixed. All agreed the right notes had been sung in the right order. Many made the point that Osbert's diction was as pellucid as ever. Some however noted a perceptible lack of any basic music in the voice.

England's oldest treble had no time to ponder reviews, far less answer the phone that screamed every five minutes. Too excited to eat breakfast, he dressed carefully in his pale grey morning suit and was away to Buckingham Palace in a taxi since parking on investiture days was an impossibility.

By midday he was posing at the gates for the evening paper photographer and joking about his television commercial. Before anyone else could suggest it, he declared his award was for Chicken Broth Efforts.

Twenty minutes later he was dead, killed outright by the unsteady driver of a pop group's van who'd ignored the traffic lights at Birdcage Walk where Osbert was crossing to a taxi.

The police found his home-help hysterical when they arrived at Osbert's open door. She'd grown fond of him in a maternal way during the ten years she'd been popping in but it was not the news of his death that she'd heard flashed on the radio that had overwrought her. It was the discovery of a cold fifteen year old boy naked in the empty bath with a large bag of mixed herbs slung round his neck.

Osbert's Regency villa is still empty if you're in a position to buy. I went to look at it myself and quite charming I thought it was in its very English way. The chrysanthemums unfortunately – and the tubs — have gone. When the police lads went back in the afternoon they did for them I'm afraid. Beneath those splendid gold blooms were six plastic bags. In each was a small white skull: clean — without one shred of flesh or hair — as though it had been simmered for a long time.

DOWN THE CROSS

When anyone shouts between the discs, 'This place isn't the same. And the park's not what it was, either,' I more often guess he's stuck in the year before yesterday. Friends tell me I'm mobile – time-wise and socially – so if I say the Cross has changed, don't suspect me of sentimentality. Arthritis of the spirit hasn't got me. Yet.

The Cross was one pulsating subculture from the moment the last bars tipped out until dawn silhouetted office cleaners emerging through the plane trees. I'm talking about any year you care to select before the mid-Seventies and the Great Clean Up. Much more than a cruising ground it was. Opera cloaks and Burberrys flapped at the coffee-stalls against Hippies, print-workers, buskers, matelots at leaves end and all pay spent, surburban couples who'd lost last trains and East European architects or dentists on parole who'd found a flicker of night life they could afford and not scurried for last trains anyway.

The Cross – in full – was Charing Cross. Consult old tube maps to fix the station. After the Great Clean Up – the patient embourgeoisement of this cauldron of raw London – even the name was sanitised to Embankment. The reasons, but of course, were valid. An urgent need to redevelop the station. If you want to do that it follows you must close two coffee stalls and neglect to open them ever again. Add the rumour of a stabbing, top it with the tale that somebody told someone else of an attempted murder in the shrubberies and it was obvious the public spirited had to act.

I mean, people had actually been chatting the August nights away on those nearby public benches – even having it away in the said shrubberies. So the city elders caged the gardens : had them bolted after the chilly-fingered orchestras had folded the scores of My Fair Lady and shuffled away at sundown.

Basically it was the problem of people like Davie and me enjoying ourselves. Or each other. A central problem that since time was measured and enjoyment was deemed – by some – to be a waste of it. So, Sunday to Saturday, panda cars circuited that block on the hour and plodding constables went counterclockwise on the half. Yet how could people be booked for loitering (despite the lack of coffee stalls) when there were night bus stops where one and all could slide in line at the first hint of the boys in blue? Answer : move the bus stops. And they did for unassailably logical reasons. The night system bewildered tourists on whom the economy increasingly depended. Lo, all was simplified and each route started under Nelson's one good eye in well lit Trafalgar Square where his Lordship, frozen high on his plinth, poor bugger, couldn't even be heard whispering, 'Kiss me, Hardy'. Without the Cross, there'd have been no Davie. At least I'd not have met him. Let's not romanticise those early Seventies. There were discos here and there and a fistful of gay bars but they weren't Davie's scene. Not that he was closety – just sort of casually gay, business commitments permitting. Be assured there was nothing ifsy or butsy about the way we picked each other out one midnight two degrees below by the edges of the Cross.

Unlit toilets and dim orgy rooms were never my bag. For me it's faces first though I do empathise with that frisson others get from cruising the unknown. I sensed it always when heading for the Cross. Maybe that's why, half way down Villiers Street (if you're not over-familiar with London, Villiers Street commemorates King James the First's regular – the Duke of Buckingham – so one was on home ground) I paused, groping for a cigarette. No need, I found, to step out of the razoring north-easterly into a doorway. Behind the unexpected flame I took in a lean, dimpled jaw, brown hair flecked early with grey and a Scots accent. I was hooked.

We chatted with the conventional ease of regular bridge players. 'Cold night' . . . 'Far to go?' . . . 'Daft there's no all night trains' . . . 'Fancy a coffee?' . . . 'My place is less than a mile from the river'.

An unexpected hiatus then from Davie's bidding.

'I've a bit of business first if you'd no mind stepping along to the Hilton for maybe twenty minutes.'

Did I mind? With the promise of a cherries-and-cream skin that wouldn't taste like a choirboy's talcummed arse, two hours wouldn't have fretted me – more likely hyped the lust factor. To the Hilton we pushed through two-thirds of a gale.

'If this deal's successful, the cab home's on me – no argument,' Davie threw over his collar as we turned through a revolving door into the lobby.

'Christ,' I panted, 'I could do with a pee.'

'I'll second that.'

We cantered down the composite marble stairway to discover a substantial percentage of London's unattached males stricken that midnight with an epidemic of bladder trouble. Not a word had been whispered, I swear, in that echoing vault until we erupted. Glances at us from all compass points went tutt, tutt, as if our laughter had disrupted some religious rite.

There are friends and there are lovers and sometimes both I've known twenty years yet still leave an empty stall between us for decency's or prudence sake. With Davie – no such hesitation. We stood close, chatting of this and that. Yes, I was wordy, having sunk a pint or two. Not Dutch courage so I could face the Cross. No such shit – I'd been to a party : finish. Appreciate however reactions weren't as nippy as usual when I heard a metallic clatter across the tiles. The first I registered from a corner of one eye was that toilet clearing like the Police Commissioner and a wolfhound pack were swarming. When cause and evident effect connected I looked down. Close by my foot was a Luger automatic.

'Not to worry,' Davie was giggling, 'I deal in them – antique weapons for collectors. The thing's nae loaded, man.'

He scooped it from the floor and, as we regained lobby level, suggested I grab a vacant alcove by the street door and order coffee.

'I'm away up the stair,' he explained. 'Give me say ten minutes. If I come down alone it's one quick coffee – don't wait on me, bye the bye, drink your own. If I'm with anyone, not a flicker from you. Negotiations will be delicate. Home with you quick and leave me to follow when I can. Give me the address again.'

So I ordered a pot for two. Had barely finished one cigarette to be exact when Davie moved swiftly back down the staircase from the bedroom area.

'No time,' he waved as I started to pour, 'we'll away before my client changes his mind.'

In the cab we talked a bit about his daily grind at a suburban baked beans factory and his leisure, divided between trading antique firearms and work on oil paintings: landscapes mostly of the Highlands and Islands. Before he was thirty five – three summers yet – he aimed to be painting full time.

I happened to look at his lap.

'Dealing in passports, too?'

'O, these? Just minding them for a couple of contacts,' he smiled as something more than five hundred dollars and as much in French francs drifted around the cab floor.

'Uh huh,' I grunted, turning as casually as I could to squint through the rear window, having the vaguest suspicion Uncle John Mills and Uncle Trevor Howard in trench coats might be urging a police car to level with us.

'How much did you raise on the Luger?' my tone, I hoped, was artless.

Davie unbuttoned his topcoat to show the dull shape of the butt.

'I see,' I said, taking care to pay off the cab two blocks from home.

'Not slow on the uptake, are ye?' Davie joked as he realised, after a four minute walk, what I'd done.

Perhaps because I didn't reply and we, not bothering with the niceties of coffee, were undressing each other layer by layer in a slow shuffle from porch to bedroom, Davie returned to the question as we slid under the electric blanket.

'Worried?'

'A new man, a new world,' I murmured, exploring with my palm the taut globe of his scrotum. Indeed it was for, that night (well it was still dark), I slept with a Luger under my pillow.

'Maybe we shouldna meet again,' Davie ventured between bites into a fried egg sandwich. I pounced on the 'maybe' for the loving had rated ten points.

Now married insurance clerks on the hoof from debt collectors have been known to hawk themselves around the Cross, making it a Lucky Dip every night. Or not so lucky as, eg: insurance clerks weighted with tension can be a soggy banana indeed despite the comfort of an electric blanket. Not so with Davie. As noted, he was for me, ten points.

'What's all this "maybe"? You know the address and there's the phone. What's yours?'

'The Grey Lion'll do fine. Let the barman know you've been in . . .' Well, there was a bar that wouldn't have turned gay if five thousand activists with banners brave and fluttering had thrust through the Public and out the Saloon doors. 'Seriously man,' he was wiping up the last of the yolk as he spoke, 'my world's nae yours. Couldna' do you any good in a respected job like your own. Might even get you on a police file.'

'Listen. There are files on one in ten of London's population. If I'm not listed already I want to know why the hell not with all the taxes they extort for law and order. Maybe – (I banked on that unloaded Luger and no psychotic gleam in Davie's eye) – maybe it's you who's fretting a bit about respectability. O yes, let the world suppose you do the fucking and, voilà, man or woman – where's the difference – you can still face the neighbours. So how do you face them this morning, after last night?'

'Bollocks to that, man,' Davie coughed on the cigarettes he was lighting for us both. 'I've had sessions with headshrinkers like the rest in Approved Schools. You mate, turned me on, not any bloody environment you come from No one fucks Davie Forbes into respectability so you can forget all that.'

'Wouldn't dream of trying,' I grinned. He was right though.

One early warning of respectability is predictability. Davie could count (and he soon sussed it) on my being at this bar or that coffee shop at such a time or day. More often than not he stood me up. Weeks elapsed between meetings. Not that I aimed at steering him to any responsibility to me. I showed none to him. There were others (though I admit I gave the Cross a miss) and – to me – a shared bed was more important just then than it ever seemed to Davie.

Yet there was affection and respect; casually shown, never discussed. Nothing in the apartment was ever lifted. I marked his birthday with a commonplace lighter since he'd sold his own that came from better-not-ask. That was in a week when the baked beans – if they existed beyond his sales patter – weren't paying well and paintings, passports and firearms were at a disheartening low. That Christmas Eve he produced a silver pistol in bed.

'Belonged to Lord Byron,' he claimed/improvised, whichever you choose, 'Historical junk's more your line than mine. Might remind you of me,' he giggled dropping it on my chest.

'Christ, I'm glad you're not as bloody chilly to the touch.'

One weekend I calculated I'd not seen Davie for a couple of months. Better weather I thought, wondering if he was after a new season's pickings by the sea. Held in London by my job, I envied him those prosperous shores of Brighton or Torquay or wherever he'd most likely set up. Maybe, with his stumbling French, he's trying (I speculated) the Riviera League.

Had it not been for a greengrocer given to wrapping carrots in yellowing newsheets I'd not have seen Davie's mugshot in the paper. Three months for robbery and brandishing an empty Luger menacingly. I tried – all discreetly – to locate which prison; sent a non-committal note but got no reply. It was around then I changed my job and the apartment, too, but not my habit of an occasional cruise around the Cross once I'd unpacked my discs and a pissy-wet Spring gave way to hot July nights.

No use by then asking Harry at the newstand if Davie had been about – which he could have been with remission for comformist behaviour. Harry was new: remembered no-one. It was closing time, too true, for the great pleasure garden of the Cross. Only the

98

dirty dozen stank in their boxes under the railway arch. Among them trotted researchers from television and debutantes with a conscience carrying small bowls of soup and large questionnaires. The Cross had altered.

Last Saturday it was, after the old girls' funeral. I was tarting up for a party. Not that I'd know her or anyone else in the block enough to attend the service. Clubbed with the neighbours for a wreath and left the relatives to cope with the rest and round off the day with a nice bit of ham and salad. Barely out of the shower I was when the yelling started. I presumed it would be the bereaved discussing some finer points of the Will. When no-one damped it down and I could hardly catch the early news for the noise I opened my door onto the landing. A tipsy woman in sober hat and coat was berating a clergyman.

'And I'll say it again . . . you're a bloody vulture. Round here before the dirt's settled on her head giving out you want bits for your church raffle. That's a bleeding jardiniere that is – and you know it. Worth a hundred any day up West, is that . . . and my kids need shoes. You and yer raffles. Bloody whisky more like. I can smell it on yer now . . .'

'Will you listen a moment, lassie . . .'

No gloomy landing could distort that voice and – despite the grubby dog-collar – I knew that lean and dimpled chin.

'When you've a moment, father,' I began and the Reverend Davie turned with a spark in his eye. 'I've a small silver pistol that might be of interest to you, when you've a moment.'

'And just watch he doesn't con you, mate,' spat the mourner, slamming the door.

'A silver pistol,' Davie mused stepping into my apartment. 'You came by it in a legitimate way of course, my son?'

'Indeed father,' I'd grabbed him by both shoulders, 'from a man who shared my bed. It belonged to Lord Byron. He was a non-conformist, too, so it is in the right hands.'

Davie, playing my spine with his fingers like a xylophone, whispered, 'Fancy a drink down the Cross tonight?'

'Where can you have been, father? The Cross is as smart as a

Chelsea Square these nights . . .'

'Then we'd better entertain ourselves at home eh? We could start with a drink,' he began to prise at my lips with his tongue as he spoke, 'later,' he mumbled as I was undoing his dog-collar.

FLICKERING SHADOWS

Only a youth of rare heroism would have mentioned twenty years ago – just as an afterthought to any prospective landlady – 'Incidentally, I prefer men in bed'. No doubt there were – here and there – sophisticated householders with paisley shawls tossed over the stairs and lacquered fans displayed in the bathroom who might not have blanched. Most would have shrieked, 'Angels and Sunday papers preserve us' and hustled such an intrepid pioneer out into the rain.

Dolly Saxon was not sophisticated and her prospective tenant was no dedicted forerunner of gay liberation so there was no such challenge when, on the first of September 1956, Clive Nichols paid a deposit on the ground floor front. The walls, predictably, were daffodil yellow and the paintwork a fashionable battleship grey but the soft furnishings smelt sweeter than those in any of the dozen rooms Clive had inspected. The divan was something between single and double: broad enough for overnight hospitality but sufficiently narrow to encourage intimacy given one nudge of interest on a visitor's part. It was the upright grand piano against the outer wall that clinched the matter for Clive.

Obviously Dolly found him suitable from the outset. Even as he unpacked she was confiding to a friend on the phone, 'Most acceptable. Tell you all when I see you . . . I'm certain I'll take to this one if only because . . .' Clive felt it proper to close his door. Compliments – even those not intended for his ears – embarrassed him for he had survived an emotionally undernourished upbringing with troublesome scars. Three full years it had taken at the university for him to be convinced by the handsome Ivor that he was as genuinely loved as any of us can hope to be. 'What's so marvellous about a trim figure and clear glance?' Ivor had scoffed, 'Two-a-penny they are at twenty one.' Nevertheless Clive had still been slow to accept affection, frittering many an afternoon on the bed rather than in it, despite assurances that he had the more durable assets of loyalty and simple honesty.

All that had been the day before yesterday. It was autumn again – that tiresome season for sentimentalists – and Clive returning from his job at a music publishers found his new bedsitter re-echoed that evening with the hours he'd so recently shared with Ivor. His fingerwork at the upright grand was as nimble as ever but it was idle to pretend that his own light baritone was any substitute for Ivor's. He was brushing at the tide and he knew it. Ivor had gone who could say where and he was alone.

When Dolly Saxon observed one morning, 'Don't get out very much in the evenings do you?' Clive had to admit to himself that nostalgia was not enough. A successor to Ivor had to be found. Not a replacement (he was not that foolish) but someone who might be fancied for rather different qualities. So, as he closed the front gate that late September morning, he called back nonchalantly, 'Funny you should say that – I'm meeting a college friend this evening. O.K. if he comes back for coffee?'

Waiting at the bus stop he did wonder where in the wide, grey working world he might begin. Not, he was sure, in the sleazy urinal by the market. He'd already been groped there one Sunday lunchtime by a hairy-wristed man whose lambswool scarf had slipped to reveal a clerical collar.

Slightly pissed at eleven that evening after four lagers in four unrewarding bars, Clive succumbed to a bout of doubt and self-pity. 'The myth just can't be true,' he confined to a lamp-post, 'I just don't believe I'm going through a phase. Somewhere there must be someone who isn't a hairy-wristed groper or a peroxided screamer.'

Since the lamp post didn't reply, he began to trudge home via

Riverside Walk and there found Frank posed against the parapet studying the punts and wherries already moored for winter. Clive paused nearby and opened the conversation with what he felt was an original gambit: Do you like Tchaikowsky? Have you read Walt Whitman? Know anyone who ever hitched a lift with Noel Coward? If Frank wasn't very positive in his response he was certainly keen to get out of the drizzle. To Clive's ground floor room they went.

Do remember this was Clive's first casual adventure. Naturally he contrasted it with the setting in which he'd lost his virginity. A rented room with a fitful gas-fire didn't really rate against that midsummer midnight at college when he'd thoughtfully offered Ivor his spare pair of pyjamas. Sitting silent beside a stranger on the edge of the bed Clive was tense and very aware of a full bladder. They'd scarcely draped their arms around each other's shoulders when he had to excuse himself. He left Frank removing some handsome onyx link from his shirtcuffs.

It was rather odd, thought Clive as he flushed the loo, that Frank should be so fascinated by his host's career, connections and possessions. He hoped he wasn't embarking on a relationship with a social snob.

Relaxed and randy he tiptoed to find his door fully open. Frank, dressed for departure, was buttoning his trenchcoat. Even in the murky hall he did look unnaturally wan.

'Didn't let on your room was bloody haunted, did you?'

No sooner had Clive closed the door – so Frank insisted –than the piano had transformed itself into a pianola and begun to play unaided while, from the very pillow on which the visitor had just rested his curly head, discordant raspberries had sounded.

Clive, astounded, played for time.

'Would you say the performance was of a professional standard?'

'Listen, I'm not bleeding Liberace. All I recognised was "Money Is The Root Of All Evil", speaking of which,' he added with unpleasant firmness, 'I ought to have something to cover my fare and expenses. Not much chance of another client at this time, have I?'

'Are you a male whore then?' Clive whispered, attempting to steer his guest through the outer porch.

'Well you didn't think I was giving it away, did you sunshine?'

Frank was becoming more aggressive by the second so it was timely that a soft reprise of Money Is The Root Of All Evil began to filter from Clive's room. With one quick gulp Frank sped into the rain.

Clive didn't sleep until gone three but nothing happened to shake his original impression of the room: pleasant, untroubled and congenial. He said nothing to Dolly as he stumbled, late, from the bathroom and she simply mentioned that she'd heard his college friend sprinting down the wet path for the last bus. Having considered the incident for a full week he tackled Dolly.

'Mrs Saxon, sorry, Dolly. Who had the room before me?'

'Well it was empty like from April. I did have hopes Uncle Cliff might recover but it wasn't to be. A stroke, see? Well, being Welsh I like a bit of music in the house. That's why I put "piano" as well in the paper. Uncle Cliff gave all kinds of music lessons. That what you wanted to know then?'

Since both her glance and her explanation were direct Clive was sure Dolly was concealing nothing. While he was wondering how he might broach the subject of the phantom pianist he realised Dolly was repeating a question.

'Don't you think so? A real good old overhaul it could do with.'

'You mean the piano? Well I wasn't going to suggest it because I couldn't afford . . .'

'Go on with you. That's for me to see to. I've got his number somewhere . . .'

'How old was Uncle Cliff when he died, Dolly?'

'More than seventy; must have been. Now, there's a thing. He'd have been seventy three only last week. Isn't that dreadful, me forgetting already?' If Dolly had, thought Clive, Uncle Cliff had not. Very obviously his shade had been outraged by a male tart lolling on his very own bed. Cheered by such a rational explanation, Clive trotted away that night eager to offer hospitality. He avoided Riverside Walk.

'Call me Dennis,' suggested the young man. Clive didn't quibble. He was twenty three, it was midnight and he was bored with wasting his sweetness on a stained handkerchief hidden between Grieg's *Ich Liebe Dich* and Debussy's *Nuages*. Dennis quickly made it plain that he wouldn't be repeating the visit. 'No strings,' he cautioned at the bus stop, 'Remember I said no strings,' he said again as Clive nervously lit the gasfire. Pity thought Clive then immediately recollected that the chestnut hair reminded him of Ivor. The hell with comparisons, he muttered, let's enjoy here and now.

'Why are you locking that piano?' Dennis asked.

'The dust. It's terrible. We're plagued with it here. Must be that new road they're building to the airport. Hold on, Dennis. Must leave you for a tick.' Clive scampered up to the bathroom but he'd hardly time to let his erection subside before cantering downstairs two at a time to quieten the yelps from his room that would certainly bring Dolly if not the other lodgers from their beds.

Dennis, caring little for passing neighbours and less for lodgers, was redressing at the foot of the stairs with the street door full open.

'You some kind of kink?' he hissed as Clive urged him into the frosty forecourt.

'Got wires and things to that piano have you? I'm not keen on private horror shows, love. That was a fresh pack of cigarettes being spattered round the room .. . .'

'Do calm down Dennis. I'll fetch your cigarettes . . .'

'Don't bother. Share them with your spooky friend.'

'What was the piano playing?'

'If it makes any odds it was "Where Is Your Heart" . . .'

'Interesting.'

When she brought in Clive's coffee and toast Dolly asked brightly, 'Was that the door banging just after twelve?'

'Mebbe,' Clive yawned to smother his misery. What a choice he thought for the umpteenth time: chastity, which he loathed or the bedsitter which he liked. Obviously it was one or the other. Worse still, he could perhaps have become unsuspectingly an agent and would produce manifestations wherever he went. He crunched his underdone toast and nerved himself to tell Dolly he would be leaving at the end of the month. As he licked the last of the apricot jam from his thumb she brought the morning post.

'About the piano, Clive, will it disturb you if Kevin pops over tonight to tune it?'

'Just as long as it's only me he disturbs,' Clive muttered, tearing up a postcard from Ivor that had been forwarded from college.

'You might like Kevin. Uncle Cliff always said he had great potential despite obvious disadvantages,' Dorothy smiled as she closed the door.

'All I'm short of,' Clive confided to the neighbour's cat on his window-sill, 'a blind, chatty piano-tuner with five kids and musical pretensions to support.' Kevin was not blind, not married and had a distinctively firm and colourful tenor voice. A plain-spoken lad, too, who was – within five minutes – intelligently critical of the way Clive had been handling some recently purchased songs.

'So how would you know? You've not been here since I moved in. Not psychic are you?'

'Heard you a couple of times from the street. Walk the dog this way for old time's sake, see?'

Kevin rested an elbow on the piano and looked speculatively at Clive.

'Something's been nagging you this past month. The singing's been tense.' Slightly huffed Clive went to make coffee. He was flabbergasted when he returned to find Kevin sprawled over the divan.

'Made yourself quite at home then?'

'Always was a comfy divan,' Kevin replied lightly.

'Used to take a little rest between lessons with Uncle Cliff?'

Clive wondered if he was being given the come-on. As he poured the coffee and Kevin watched him, he considered whether Uncle Cliff might have been some withered Victorian, torn between inhibition and desire, daring to pat Kevin on the head but nothing more. It would be a key to recent happenings. A neurotic ghost outraged that his room, heavy with unfulfilled longing, had passed to a generation with a less arthritic love life. He can have it back, too, Clive concluded, at the end of the month. 'Sorry, Kevin, you were saying . . .?'

'I said, Yes we did both rest here, if that's what you want to call it. I'd have been seventeen when things sort of started. Cliff's lessons were free from then on, goes without saying. I came back because I wanted to though. Would have done anything for the old boy; I'm like that. If I take to someone, I stick. No pissing around on the side. It's me artisan stock, Cliff reckoned. Wouldn't you like to put your feet up too instead of wandering round like a fart in a colander?'

Kevin eased across the divan, nearer the wall. Clive perched on the edge. The piano was silent. Kevin lit cigarettes for them both. The packet was not whirled away up the chimney. Their fingers touched; then locked. Not even one muted raspberry ruffled the feather pillows.

Clive didn't sleep very much that night either. Kevin woke twice. The second time, as they were dozing, he pulled Clive's ear.

'Want to see me regular, do you? Well, it's no pissing about with other blokes, for a start. I should know, you know. I coped with Cliff for five years, didn't I? None of your two-timing or you can shag off. I'm not in the one-night stand business.'

Though they'd both been very wary of disturbing the household, Dorothy didn't bring in the breakfast tray that morning. Clive heard it being put down outside. He tiptoed across to the door without pulling the curtains and brought back the tray to the divan.

There were two mugs of coffee and some extra toast.

INVESTORS' CHRONICLE

To a foundling, curried chick-peas and uninhibited friendships need not be an irksome diet. Anthony Gamble, it must be admitted, was a foundling twice-removed. Certainly grandfather Gamble had been a doorstep bundle yet, through that dogged application so applauded by the bourgeoisie, he'd prospered in the sale of trusses or – as The Times obituary had it – gentlemens' supports.

Anthony's father deployed much of his inheritance in staging musicals. Though the chorus – in boaters and sunbonnets – cheerfully promoted the values of an England fit for Mary Whitehouse to live in, they did not for some reason pack the aisles. What money remained dribbled away on trinkets for the nicer type of whore who takes tea in hotels overlooking the park. So child Anthony's upbringing became progressively more spartan. Mother, by prudent housekeeping and ceaseless admonition, steered her offspring to a scholarship and an arts degree at one of our oldest provincial universities. It may have been Oxford; you might prefer it to have been Cambridge. Three years on it was all one to Mother for she was dead and Anthony had joined others similarly qualified in a commune financed by the Department of Social Security.

With Mother little more than a cooling memory of pig's trotters and egg-custard and Father stumbling over cider bottles in the city's twilight zones, how else could Anthony describe himself to his shaving mirror and to others but as an orphan – maturer than most at twenty five – but, an orphan. Does this suggest a romantic disposition? So be it. Who but a giant can withstand those formative undergraduate summers of peaches and religious doubts for breakfast; those will-he, won't-she midnights of champagne and precarious fumblings in a punt? Anthony was no giant – indeed was more average than his clothes proclaimed.

As he loitered in his post-graduate squat there was time enough to dream. He considered any path that might meander, legally or illegally, from curried chick-peas to a penthouse glowing with silk and money. To be mercenary was acceptable: to become a mercenary entailed hazards that bordered distastefully on excess. Rich widows were not his bag and neither his face nor his arse fitted him, he supposed, to be a statesman's rent-boy.

Resolved on action at last, Anthony dropped in on his college acquaintance Richard Scales. If nothing else, our better universities do provide a life-long contacts book any gossip columnist might envy. Richard, who was applying poise, charm and a first class degree in moral philosophy to the craft of public relations, still found Anthony as fanciable as when they had once read alternate lines of the Poet Laureate's memorable lyrics. Anthony's squash racquet and cases were stored in Richard's spare room and he still had hopes that Anthony might join them. Evading an innocent suggestion that he might stay the night, Anthony dropped in from time to time to use the flat as a changing room. Once again in paisley tie and graduation suit, he kicked his frayed denims into a corner, kissed Richard on the forehead and scurried away through the empty street to Beckfords.

Many of our gay clubs, as both patrons and members of the Vice Squad would confirm, have been lucratively modelled on the Black Hole of Calcutta. Beckfords was exceptional. Much more spacious and gracious. Among its Doric pillars and cautious lighting, almost all the patrons looked young and those who didn't looked influential. Just what Anthony himself was seeking when he first arrived we can't be certain for he himself wasn't sure.

And then he glimpsed Cherubino Surface. It was reciprocal lust at first sight. Sufficiently scrubbed to thrill a drill sergeant, clean-vowelled enough to seduce the Conservative Party, Cherubino appeared irresistible. Indeed, Anthony trusted the expensive cut of the lad's suit might conceal a flush of credit cards.

They smiled, they spoke and, long after midnight they were dancing with increasing intimacy to the admiration of all.

'O Ant,' murmured Cherubino, 'if only I could say let's drift away to my place. It is mine, you understand, but I've an insufferably protective guardian. Just imagine, if I post a letter, he tracks me with binoculars.'

'The creature's a Bluebeard,' fumed Anthony, frustrated that he could scarcely offer his own cheerless attic on the unmentionable side of the river.

'Not that he'll have any legal hold over me much longer. I do see of course that I mustn't be exposed to any unsuitable influences. The Trustees wouldn't approve.'

To Anthony, who knew a pricey after shave when he sniffed one (and he'd sniffed a fair few) mention of Trustees confirmed his luck while stoking his frustration. Excusing himself while Cherubino bought more drinks, he rang Richard's flat. The inconsiderate peasant was not in or not answering. It was a moment for improvisation.

'Which evening could you come to supper Cherubino? I've a little place by the Stock Exchange. Or I shall have, from tomorrow, when I move in.'

'Why not a week tonight? Wednesday?'

'A whole seven days? Can't I ring you? Maybe take you to a wholesome concert by Cliff Richard?' Anthony was contemplating with glum foreboding a further seven evenings of ill-digested chickpeas.

'Wednesday it must be. The only night I can escape Bluebeard's Castle. I have an arrangement with a remote great-uncle. As a child I interrupted his impersonation of a wardress seducing a High Court judge. I'm at his house now, if you see what I mean.'

For another hour Cherubino and Anthony danced on in their licentious way, that is, not quite as closely as team-mates clutch the centre-half who scores their winning goal. Their leave-taking was long and fond as they waited for Cherubino's taxi. When they reached the river bank Anthony said, 'I'll get out here. I want to walk until dawn so that I can plan everything for next Wednesday.'

And Cherubino slid away into the drizzle. Richard agreed to lend his flat, sighing that his only happiness was in knowing that Anthony would be happy. It was not difficult to exploit the warmth of the moment by asking for a loan of ten pounds and a very firm assurance that Richard would not creep home until the Thursday morning.

Not until ten past seven that crucial Wednesday evening did Anthony even consider that Cherubino might not show up. Whole tower-blocks of fantasy crumbled about his shoulders. What of his plan to move in on the lad the very night he was twenty one? (This date was calculated out of deference to the Trustees rather than the law). And, if no Cherubino, then no winter skiing and no summer yacht. A beige tomorrow of chick-peas and consciousness-raising surged in him like a belch. At a quarter-past seven the ski-slopes shimmered once more for Cherubino was in the doorway. So consumed with preparations had Anthony been and so apprehensive of the outcome that he's already smoked more than half his pack of cigarettes and knew he would never last the evening. Borrowing Richard's milk-money and leaving his guest to pick a disc, he sped in search of a corner shop that might still be open.

'O Ant,' murmured Cherubino, hearing the bell, 'how unworldly you are. You've forgotten your key.'

'Took a chance you might be in,' began the man at the door, 'the wife's in the car with a carton of chop suey. Just about time for a quickie if we're sharp about it.'

'Are you quite certain this is . . .'

'Don't piss about. If you'd sent the photo as requested I'd have found time to drop in before this. Right little darling you are, straight up. Where's your toilet?'

'Through there.'

Cherubino, saddened by the evident infidelity of his new found Anthony decided he would not stamp out immediately and make for Beckfords. He would stand his ground, confront Anthony with the curiously tatooed man in the bobble cap and then leave them to it.

'Righty,' called the voice behind him, 'let's be having you then.'

Cherubino inspected with bewilderment the bobble cap, the rope coiled about the man's waist, the mauve lacquered boots and the old paint-tin that slopped melting ice cream.

'Come on then. Let's get on with it,' the man urged, smearing his genitals with a palmful of melting vanilla. When the doorbell sounded a second time he snapped, 'expecting someone?'

'Perhaps it's your wife.'

'Not a chance. She'll linger over the bean-sprouts. Always leaves them till last.'

'It could be my friend.'

'Friend is it? Been winding me up then, have you? Who said he was lonely in the advert? Who was into mountaineering, eh? What you running here – a fourpenny brothel? Let me tell you, mate, I'm into one-to-one relationships, none of your bourgeois promiscuity.'

Cherubino, having opened the door, barred Anthony's way.

'I think, Ant,' he said, in quietly wounded tones, 'you own me an explanation.'

'I see it all,' Anthony improvised, taking in the third man at a glance. 'We've not been introduced,' he smiled. This would have been difficult on any formal basis for the stranger's hands as well as his abdomen dripped melting ice cream.

'You no doubt took Cherubino for the previous owner of the flat. Drop in next week and you'll meet Richard Scales in the flesh. He'll be round to pick up any mail . . .'

'I'm not anyone . . .'

'I'm certain you could be a cultivated taste . . .'

'Listen. I've read about this troilism lark in my Sunday paper. I've always held we progressives should adapt to the prevailing climate so what about . . .'

'Next Wednesday if you don't mind.'

Cherubino was silent while the man dressed and remained so when the door had banged behind him.

'I'd no idea you were looking for someone on a casual basis, Ant,' he sighed, 'I was beginning to think of Wednesday as our night. How youthful and idealistic I must appear.'

'Nonsense, Cherub. Of course we'll be here next Wednesday. Richard can cope with his wretched mountaineer.'

'Who is this Richard anyway? I admit this apartment is very special but I do hope those chrysanthemums are his choice. They do so point to a middle-class mind.'

'Richard was with me at the University. He's gone into Public Relations.'

'I believe my guardian is or was in something like that . . .'

'Now Cherub, forget Bluebeard. Come and tell me more about you while I open the lobster soup.'

Their meal was as exotic as an upmarket take-away could provide and their love-making which followed was so flawless and so satisfying that any description would be banal as a text-book diagram by comparison. At three in the morning, Cherubino dressed and left Anthony sleeping. He woke at eight as the faithful Richard brought in some coffee.

'All went well Ant?'

'Fine . . . and you?'

'You may well be in luck – about this flat I mean. Now you know I expected to spend the evening exploring a possible consortium? Well, amazing scenes, dear Ant, there was a personal development too. D'you know, until last night, I'd never an inkling that any man over forty could be as winsome as his cheque book.'

'Then you'd better keep very quiet about your mountaineering friend who came stamping round here,' smirked Anthony. 'Who's been advertising in the more interesting columns of the trade papers then? Anyway, be warned that your mountain goat will be prancing in here next Wednesday before his wife goes to bingo. And I'm keen to ask Cherubino over for supper again. I do apologise, in the understandable heat of the moment Richard I forgot to ask him for that ten pounds back. Never mind, next Wednesday I'll certainly discuss taking over the flat with him. Think you could make the ten pounds twenty? Just till next week?

Well, fifteen then. You're a real chum.'

'We could have a memorable dinner party next week,' Richard suggested, 'your new friend and mine I mean.'

Anthony finished his coffee with a gulp and shook his head.

'Cherubino and I need to be alone,' he simpered romantically and cuddled the empty pillow.

'Why not have the bedroom for an hour before supper then you'll both be less pent-up? The French manage these things so much more smoothly and now we're in the Common Market we should profit by their example. Fuck before frolic and all that.'

'There's gallic elegance for you,' yawned Anthony. 'What's he like, your friend?'

'Sir Julian?'

'A knight? What a furtive little social ferret you are. A captain of industry, is he? Something thrusting, white-hot and abrasive? I'm speaking of his business habits.'

'I told you but you were simpering over that pillow. He heads a public relations firm. He's hired to give a better image to arms manufacturers or porn merchants . . . maybe both, I'm not clear on the niceties. Anyway he's liberal in everything except dogs. Can't bear them. I suspect he had a wounding experience.'

Seven evenings later, Cherubino and Anthony rested again on that very divan in Richard's spare room. They had made love twice and when Anthony was roused to further enthusiasm, Cherubino groped for the cigarettes.

'Do you think, dear Ant,' he whispered, circling a forefinger around Anthony's sensitive navel, 'that I might move in here with you soon?'

'Tomorrow?'

'Well, let's not put a date on it. I'm almost twenty one now. To tell you the truth Bluebeard is having delusions about me again.'

'Then the sooner we whisk you out of the monster's castle the better. Say next week?'

'Could be. And Ant . . . I hardly like to ask . . . could you stake me, in a modest way of course, for a couple of months? Just until my birthday. Bluebeard might try to hold up my allowance. I am a simple soul. I mean a hundred a week would be more than ample for fritter money.'

Anthony gulped. Happily, a crescendo of pneumatic bliss could be heard from the other bedroom and they were both distracted by it.

'Is the mountaineer having trouble with his crampons do you suppose?' Cherubino giggled.

'Possibly. But our Richard appears to have more of a bulging social diary than I suspected. That could well be Sir Julian floundering to a peak.'

'Sir who?'

'Julian Exwoth. I, well, allowed Richard to entertain him here, you see, but we won't have to suffer the noises off much longer. Richard is moving in on the dear knight any day.'

'Is he just,' snapped Cherubino snatching at his underpants.

'What's wrong Cherub? There's a tightness about your lips I've not noticed before.'

'I fear you have deceived a simple youth Anthony. Mountaineers who pop in for quickies. College friends who use your flat as a knocking-shop. And now, Julian Exworth in the next room.'

'You know him?'

'Julian, my friend, is Bluebeard,' Cherubino hissed, disarranging his curls with care. As they emerged, Cherubino ready for off, Anthony swathed in a bath towel bordered with Spartan warriors and frantic, the doorbell sounded. Richard darted from the main bedroom.

'So this,' he smiled hopping naked across the lounge towards the hall,' is Cherubino.'

'Three of you this time, is it?' whistled the man in the bobble cap,' And not even the decency to dim the lights. Bloody bourgeois depravity. Mind if the bloodhound has a drop of water?'

'Do feel free,' Richard called after the man who'd already made for the kitchen.

'Whore, promiscuous two-timing trollop, liberated slut,' boomed an amply proportioned gentleman who stood, in Jaeger socks and orange suspenders by the door of the main bedroom.

'Shit,' moaned Cherubino, 'Julian.'

'Four's coming it a bit,' said the man in the bobble cap, removing his mauve boots, 'I've a mandatory shop-stewards meeting first thing in the morning I'd have you know.'

Anthony dropped a protective arm round Cherubino who shivered as he mumbled, 'O dear God.'

'Indeed, I have been that and more,' yelled Sir Julian, scooping up a wolfskin rug and twining it round his loins. Then he confronted Anthony. 'Whoever you may be, you're welcome to that expensive little tart. Cherubino? Is that what he's calling himself? Before I befriended him, rigged him out, sent him for speech lessons with an underpaid telecaster, what was he I'd like to know? Well, what were you, you Don Juan of the hot-dog stalls? An out-of-work waiter hawking your tiny magic flute along the river bank, that's what you were. And to think what I've done for you out of the kindness of my heart: didn't I get you the best velour trilby money could buy?'

'It was two sizes too small,' protested Cherubino.

'No doubt you wouldn't have minded arriving at the races looking like a Jewish bookie?'

'Thought you told me your wife was Jewish?' Richard interrupted.

'Until I was knighted, so she was. She's managed to adapt very quickly to black puddings and cosubstantiation. Kindly don't interrupt, Richard.'

'I like a bloke with a neat turn of phrase,' said bobble cap, advancing on Sir Julian.' Naturally you're a crypto-fascist. I might stretch a point though. Fancy a quickie? Both sides of industry should come together for the good of the country.' Sir Julian, however, was scrambling via a chair to the dining table, leaving the wolfskin between the bloodhound's teeth. Concealing his genitals with a napkin he screamed, 'Get that rabid hound away from me. Must I have my image savaged by dogs until I haven't a leg to stand on?'

'I think you,' said Richard calmly to bobble cap, 'should piss off to your wife. You and I, Julian, should head for your place. And you two lovers had best untangle your finances and your fantasies. If you can afford this flat *and* Cherubino, Anthony, move in when you wish.'

'Not Cherubino,' sighed Sir Julian adjusting his napkin, 'his name is Len.' When the three others had gone, Antony fetched champagne from the kitchen.

'We must try to make it last. There'll be no more, Cherubino.'

'That's true. And I am Len. I've deceived you Ant.'

'And I you. This isn't my flat. I live in a commune; a squat.'

'I shall have to go back to washing the plates of rich tourists Ant.'

'It's chick-peas and consciousness-raising for me.'

'You don't think, do you, that I could come too?'

'I can only offer self-awareness, experimental curries and space in an attic overlooking Gasworks Lane.'

'With you thrown in, it would be luxury. After all, basically, I'm only a foundling on the make.'

'Aren't we all?' laughed Anthony, filling their glasses with such vigour that his towel dropped to the floor.' I'm a foundling myself, well, twice-removed.'

Other Works By Peter Robins

Undo Your Raincoats And Laugh
Available from Brilliance Books £1.50 post paid

The Gay Touch
Crossing Press U.S.A.

Other stories

Cracks In The Image
Gay Men's Press U.K.

On The Line
Crossing Press U.S.A. British Distributers 'Airlift'

Also from Brilliance Books

Undo Your Raincoats And Laugh Peter Robins
'Pure irony, refreshingly unmoralised'
Times Literary Supplement

Three Rainbows Tenebris Light
'An avant garde collection of stories expressing the fantasy and
reality of the gay experience'

Brilliance Books wishes to thank the Gay Men's Press for their
constant support and solidarity

Brilliance Books is a totally gay imprint and welcomes
manuscripts from gay writers